THE HOTEL AT BEACH AND FORGOTTEN

NELLIE BROOKS

Merpaper Press LLC

Edited by Karen Meeus Editing

Published by Merpaper Press LLC

CONTENTS

CHAPTER 1

"W hatever you do, don't tell the kids. I don't want them to know I lost the house." Jenny's voice echoed in the empty living room. She was sitting on her packed duffle bag because it was the only thing left to sit on. The vibrant rugs and midcentury sofas, the soft leather chairs and abstract paintings were gone.

Throughout the month of May, trucks had come and gone between the house and who knew where. Everything that could be repossessed had been repossessed. From the family's barbecue set by the pool to the carefully curated knickknacks of twenty-five years, Jenny's life in Portland, Maine, had been wrapped up and carried off, one memory at a time.

All that was left was her packed bag, a few things without value like her and Stan's old marriage bed, and Jenny herself.

She shifted her cell phone to her other ear. "Glenn? Can you please do that for me?"

"What do I say if Audrey asks me straight out where you are?" Glenn wanted to know. "I get nervous when I have to lie, and your kids are too smart not to notice."

"For now, just tell them I'm on vacation." Jenny scratched her knee. She wasn't all alone in the big empty house, after all—the mosquitoes were still here too. One was whirring next to her ear, and she waved it away. "It's not much of a lie since I meant to visit Mendocino Cove for years. Say I wanted to see my childhood home again; just don't mention why. Can you do that for me?"

"I'll do anything for you." Glenn sounded more critical than devoted. "You know I will. But lying by omission is still lying, Jenny. It's a whopper, too."

"Believe me, it's for the best. I would do anything for the kids, and right now, they need to not worry about me. Let me get straightened out before I tell them what's going on."

Jenny waited for Glenn to agree. She needed an official *yes* to trust him, even though he had been a good friend for over twenty years. But Stan had been her best friend, and she'd trusted him more than anyone.

Stan had claimed he would do anything for her. *Anything.* Then, a year ago, he checked into the swanky Portland Harpoon, ordered champagne, and used it to wash down a bottle of prescription sleeping pills.

To say Jenny had trust issues would be an understatement.

"I won't tell the kids, Jenny," Glenn promised.

She exhaled a tense breath. "Thanks, Glenn."

"That said, I still think you should tell your kids what's happening, Jenny. You're their mother. Don't you think they have a right to know how you are?"

"I'm perfectly fine. That's all they need to know." Relieved, Jenny stood from her crouched seat and stretched her legs.

It was barely seven in the evening, but even though it was already May, it was getting dark outside. Would the lights come on when she flipped the switch? She hadn't paid the bill, and the power company must be catching on.

"Oh come on, you're not *fine*, Jen," Glenn said patiently. "You are completely broke."

"It's all right. I'll get a job. I have a degree."

"Don't mind me saying this, but it's been a while since you've worked."

Glenn wasn't wrong.

Jenny had loved doing her thesis research on the island of Nantucket, and she had published in high-ranking academic journals. But when Stan asked her to marry and move to Maine with him, she never looked back.

"Maybe it's been a hot second," Jenny conceded.

"Besides, how many paying jobs are there for historians?"

"I'm sure there are *some*."

"How long do you plan on waiting for one of them to come along?"

She cleared her throat. "Glenn. I can find something else. Maybe I could work as an administrative assistant."

Glenn's voice was gentle. "Forgive me for saying this, my dear, but at our age, getting *any* job is hard. We're in our midforties and no longer spring chickens. You look fantastic, of course. Not a day past twenty-two."

"Of course." Jenny sighed. A whole lot of good that did her.

"I'm just trying to be real about—"

"What do you want me to say, Glenn?" Jenny broke in. "The kids can't help me. They already have to deal with too much."

"But—"

"I know it's been a year, but believe me when I say River and Audrey are still very much dealing with losing their dad. I do not want them to worry about me when they can do nothing to fix my situation anyway." She stopped talking and swallowed the icy lump of panic rising from her chest into her throat. Unlike actual ice, it went back down like sandpaper. "I tried to talk Audrey into taking a year off to take care of herself. But she wanted the schoolwork to keep her busy. It's how she copes."

"Aha," said Glenn. "Coping by staying busy. Like mother, like daughter."

"I worry about Audrey. Cornell's hotel management program is terribly competitive. It was a stressful semester, and now her finals are coming up."

Glenn hummed his concern. "Has she complained?"

"Of course not." Jenny sighed. "Now there's a mother-daughter example for you. She won't tell me anything because *she's* scared *I* will crack."

"You're not cracking, are you?"

The outburst came out of nowhere. "I'm not Stan, am I? I didn't sell out my family to hide my shady business dealings." The icy ball was back, blocking her windpipe. Jenny gasped for breath like a fish out of water.

There was a moment of silence.

Then, "You know that's not what I meant," Glenn said gently.

"Sorry. I'm sorry for snapping at you, Glenn. I'm so sorry."

He hummed forgiveness. "Don't worry, I can take a snap here and there. It was a shock, wasn't it." It was a statement, not a question.

Jenny bit the raw spot inside her cheek. "I didn't see any of it coming. I don't know how to get over it. I don't seem to be healing."

"I imagine it takes time."

"The kids claim they're all right. But how good can they be?"

"I don't know," Glenn said. "*I'm* not good, and I was only Stan's friend, not family."

Jenny didn't particularly want to linger on the topic. There were days when it took all her love for the kids not to fall into the temptingly numb abyss of wine and space gummies.

"Please understand." Jenny shut her eyes so hard little bright stars popped. "If Audrey fails her exams... I can't pay for another semester. Nor can she."

"What about your son?"

Jenny pressed a hand to her chest. Pressing the vagus nerve supposedly helped calm anxiety, but maybe she wasn't doing it right. "River makes just enough to take care of himself, and he's saving what little he can to buy an engagement ring for his girlfriend. I think he needs a family of his own to make up for the one he lost. I know how that feels. I'm not going to ask him to change his plans."

"He hasn't lost his family, Jenny. River has you and Audrey, and he won't thank you for losing your house over his medical school, either."

"The house is already gone, and that tuition has long been paid too. River is in his second year of residency. He's terribly busy, too. Sometimes, he doesn't get to sleep for days."

"But what about you?"

Jenny sighed softly so he wouldn't hear. Glenn only wanted to help, but she was done discussing this. "What about me? I'm a grown woman. I'll figure it out. And I'll do it before the kids catch on."

CHAPTER 2

J enny walked to the door and flipped the switch, squinting at the ceiling. No light. No heat. But it wasn't a problem. She only had one more night in this house.

Jenny flipped the switch back off. "I don't *care* if I sleep in my car and eat canned tomatoes for the rest of my life. I'm the parent, and I'm going to smooth the waves as much as I can. At least until they graduate. Let that be my one achievement, Glenn. Do not tell them I lost the house. Do not tell them I need help. I *don't*. I need them to stay the course."

"Okay," Glenn finally relented. "Okay. You are the parent. It is your decision. I won't tell them." He, too, took a deep breath. "Where are you going to sleep tonight?"

Jenny repressed a sigh of relief. "I'll sleep here, at the house. I still have the bed upstairs."

"Heat?"

"Um."

"Come here. Stay with us. It's okay. I promise."

"Ha." Jenny smiled. "I can practically hear Kimberly roll her eyes. No, I'm all right here. I'll get in touch soon."

"Kimbie would love to have you stay with us."

Kimbie barely made it through appetizers on the rare double dates before yawning and dropping scarcely veiled hints that it was time to wrap up the evening. "Tell her thanks, but I'll have my last night in the old family home. Glenn, I gotta make another call before my battery runs out."

"Do you have any money at all?"

"I have enough to last me until I find a job."

"Your reply is worryingly unspecific. Call me tomorrow, please."

"Thank you, Glenn. For everything. I love you."

"Love you too, Jenny. Chin up, okay? Everything will work out. You'll be fine."

For a penniless widow of forty-five who'd just had her home and car repossessed, *fine* seemed unlikely. But what choice was there? "Sure. I'll be in touch. Bye, Glenn."

Jenny ended the call and pulled a tiny notebook from the pocket of her jeans. It used to be her mother's. The palm-sized, dog-eared pages were yellow and brittle with age but faithfully held the phone numbers of three generations.

She quickly found the number she wanted and walked to the window for more light.

The back yard was just starting to turn green. In the summer, the mature trees and bushes would hide the carefully restored roofs of the neighboring pre-Civil War homes.

As if to mock her, rain started rapping at the window. The staccato sound was loud without the furniture to muffle it.

"April showers bring May flowers," Jenny whispered, and then she tapped the number on the phone screen. "Here goes nothing."

"Yeeees?" The short word was luxuriously drawn out, the voice immediately recognizable.

"Aunt Georgina? Is that you?" Relief washed through Jenny. It was so good to hear that voice.

"Jenny? Darling! What are you—I can't believe you are calling me! What a surprise!" Someone laughed in the background, and a band was playing an old Tom Ford hit.

"*I* can't believe you still have the same number." They only talked once in a blue moon.

"I know! I forever lose my phones and think now they'll give me a new one, but they never seem to change—Hang on, honey. It's so... Hey! Can you all be quiet? Be quiet. It's my niece. I want to talk to her."

"Where are you, Aunt Georgie?" Jenny closed her eyes to feel closer to her aunt. She had sent Georgie an email about Stan six months before. But Georgie didn't email back. She never did. Jenny wasn't sure Georgie ever saw her emails.

"I'm in the Bahamas! Can you imagine? It's marvelous. Blue water and palm trees and, uh, coconuts."

"Coconuts?"

"Yes, on the breakfast buffet. They bring them in the little boats going between the cruise ship and the islands."

"Are you with Fred?"

"Listen, honey, I *love* you. But this isn't really a *good* time to talk. Everyone is a bit tipsy, and we *just* got our dessert. Why are you calling?"

It was never a good time to talk for Auntie Georgie. She was forever busy having fun with, or mourning the demise of, her latest profitable marriage.

"I was wondering about the old family hotel in Mendocino," Jenny said bravely. "I was wondering if it's still standing."

"Of course it's still there. At least I think so. I haven't been to California in a while. What about the hotel, honey?"

"I lost my husband and my house," Jenny admitted. "I need a place to stay where I can get back on my feet."

"Oh, honey! It's that dreadful man you married, isn't it? Steven? It's Steven's fault, isn't it?"

"Stanley. He passed away a year ago, Aunt Georgie." Jenny mentally crossed her fingers. "Would you mind if I stayed at the hotel in Mendocino for a while?"

"I don't think it'll be much fun, sweetheart," Georgie said skeptically. "I've all but *forgotten* about that place. It's probably all dusty. Are you sure?"

"I'm sure."

"Well, okay." The vowels were drawn out, long and luscious. "Do you have a key?"

Jenny tucked her chin. "Do you mean to say you've never changed the locks?"

"The locks?" Georgie chuckled. "Who would want to break in? Everyone either forgets the place exists or thinks it is haunted. You know—by ghosts."

"There's no such thing as ghosts, Auntie. I don't believe in any of that. I'm happy to stay there."

"Well, it's probably okay if you don't have anything better. All the furniture and things should still be there."

"Did you have a company take care of the house?"

"Yes, but they don't dust, only make sure there aren't any cracked windows or burst pipes or birds stuck in the chimney. At least I can stop paying for that service if you're in the house."

"Of course. I'll take care of everything. Including the dusting."

That cheered her aunt up. "You know what? If I have to call the company anyway, I'll ask them to make sure to switch on water and electricity for you."

"Thank you, Aunt Georgie. That's very kind of you."

"I know! Well, you enjoy yourself in Mendocino. I'll see you...sometime." The laughter and music in the background became louder again.

"See you sometime, Auntie. I love you."

"I—" Georgie giggled as if someone had suddenly tickled her. The call broke off.

"*I love you too*," Jenny murmured, finishing the sentence for her aunt.

Georgina's husbands died frequently, mostly of old age, and happy to leave her plenty of money. As far as

Jenny could tell, Georgie used her inheritances to hunt in style for the next rich man willing but unable to keep up with her voluptuously narcissistic company.

Jenny lifted her phone for one last call.

"Hello? Yes. Yes, can I buy a ticket for the flight to San Francisco tomorrow morning at five-thirty? Just one. Only one way, please."

The credit card charge went through.

Jenny breathed a sigh of relief.

By the time they arrived to change the locks, she would be on her way to sunny Mendocino Cove, holding on tight to an old key.

CHAPTER 3

D riving a rental car on her own through San Francisco was something Jenny had dreaded, but
mere moments after she pulled out of the rental lot,
her anxiety dissipated like the morning fog that rolled
down the steep streets.

The GPS led her easily through wide streets with
little traffic. At one point, Jenny parked in front of a
deli and got out to buy steaming hot coffee and fresh
croissants before driving on. Soon after that, the Gold-
en Gate Bridge rose majestically before her.

Jenny rolled down her window; the air in the airport
had been stale and conditioned, and the car smelled of
the last renter's perfume. But not out here! This close
to the bay, it was breezy, and the air coming in from the
bay was as clean and clear as crystal.

A flock of seagulls swooped overhead, screaming at
the motorboats zipping like toys through the water, or
at the frolicking sea lions, or maybe the gulls screamed
out of sheer joy at the beauty of the bay.

She smiled; she was really starting to enjoy herself. It
was a proper San Fran morning, and the cool slipstream
of Jenny's car nipped at her skin even though she was

wearing her favorite cashmere sweater. She touched the small hole near the sleeve.

Her dearly missed friend, Barney, had ripped it into the soft fabric. Barney was the golden retriever she'd adopted in college. Unfortunately, Stan and Barney didn't take to each other, and when Barney died, Stan bought new couches and announced they were to have no more animals in the house.

Jenny bought the kids hamsters anyway, causing her and Stan's first marital spat. Stan needed a night in the Harpoon to calm down. When he finally returned home, he brought chocolates for the kids and for her, a bowl with a goldfish swimming in it. Jenny named her fish Lady Valentia and faithfully changed its water for a year before a marauding cat jumped through an open window into the kitchen and ate it.

At a traffic light, Jenny pulled out the hair tie holding her messy top bun and shook out her shoulder-length hair. The salty air tugged the tangled strands free and washed the long airplane ride off her skin.

"Wish you could be here with me, Stan," Jenny whispered and leaned closer to the steering wheel to see the top of the iconic landmark.

Even though it was still cool, the breeze had blown away the fog. The bright morning sun streamed through the windows, giving the red bridge a fiery golden hue. Jenny put on her sunglasses and crossed the bridge, smiling from ear to ear. When she reached the other side, she pulled into a lookout spot to get out of the car and properly admire the gorgeous view.

"Having a good day?" An aging hippie with long dreadlocks and a graying beard smiled at her.

Jenny hadn't seen him sitting on one of the boulders behind the bench where she sat. "Yes." She returned the smile. "How about you?"

"Always." He looked back at the golden-red bridge, the azure sky, and the sapphire water. "Yes," he murmured. "Always." He pulled his legs higher, hugging them for warmth.

"Would you like coffee?" Jenny asked. "It's only black, but it's hot."

His eyes lit up. "You have coffee?"

"Give me a moment." Jenny fetched the cup and croissant from her car and, when she was back, handed them to the old man.

"You don't want it?" He reached for the breakfast she was holding out.

She shook her head. "I'm not hungry, and I'm not cold, and I certainly don't need caffeine after this view."

"Cool." He laid the paper bag on his knees and pried open the lid with tanned hands that looked surprisingly young, inhaling the steam that curled into the air. "You be happy too, lady." He winked at her. "Be happy like me: *always*."

"Got it." Jenny winked back and returned to her bench, where she snapped a cute picture of herself, grinning and with windblown hair, the Golden Gate Bridge glowing like melted gold in the Californian sun behind her.

Then she wrote an email each to River and Audrey on the phone, telling them she was taking a well-deserved vacation to visit her beloved childhood home in Mendocino Cove, which was at the coast and the most beautiful place she knew.

Audrey texted back immediately, sounding relieved that Jenny was having fun. Jenny looked at the text for a long time, touching the words with her finger as if it brought her daughter closer.

River wouldn't write back until the evening or the next day. Maybe even the day after that. He answered emails and texts only when he had time to do so, but the important part was that he did answer.

Jenny shivered when she finally tucked her phone away. The old hippie was gone, but he'd forgotten the empty bakery bag where he sat, weighed down with a stone. Jenny picked the bag up and tossed it in the garbage bin by the parking lot. A Japanese tourist with a bucket hat and Capri pants was doing the same thing at the same time, and they smiled at each other before returning to their respective cars.

Back in the driver's seat, Jenny put the heat on to warm up and drove off the scenic hill with the vista point. Once she was back on the highway, traffic thickened. Jenny listened to music and patiently followed the stop-and-go-flow, drifting along.

There was so much to see even here, in the middle of what seemed to be a fourteen-lane highway. A mother and daughter laughing in the beat-up Tesla beside her, a young man blaring music in an open Audi convertible, a brown Lincoln that seemed to have no driver at all, so short were they. Often, Jenny's gaze wandered to the side of the highway where the golden-grassed hills rose soft and steep. She had missed them. Sometimes, she had seen them in her dreams.

CHAPTER 4

S tan preferred skiing in Canada and Colorado or cruises to Caribbean and European hot spots. Mendocino Cove was too small and much too out of the way for him. There'd been an unspoken promise that they would visit Jenny's hometown when he retired and had more time. Or at least Jenny had thought it had been an unspoken promise.

How many of their fancy trips had Stan financed with money that wasn't his? The thought knotted Jenny's stomach. She swallowed down the grief, her unresolved anger, and her fear of the future.

They could have been fine.

They could easily have lived in a smaller house and stayed in Portland for their vacations. There were several beautiful beaches in and around the city. Gorgeous Acadia National Park had practically been a stone's throw away—a couple of hours driving, if that. It was good enough for tourists from all over the world. It would have been more than enough.

For Jenny.

Not, apparently, for Stan. The man she'd lived with for the last twenty-seven years and knew not at all.

Breathing deep, Jenny tried the vagus nerve again but again could tell no difference.

The traffic thinned more and more until there were few other cars on the road. The rolling hills were sparingly dotted with ranches and oak trees, sun-dried wood fences, black cattle and brown horses.

The air grew warmer and the sun brighter. Jenny had long since switched off the heat, and now she rolled her window down. It wasn't enough, so she stopped to wiggle out of her sweater before driving on. The Mamas and Papas were playing on the radio, and when her favorite song came on, Jenny leaned her arm on the open window and sang the words out loud into the warm wind.

She made another couple of stops, one at a roadside fruit stand where she bought a small basket of apples and one in Santa Rosa, where she ate a cheeseburger and fries at a pretty diner.

Jenny was wiping her fingers on a paper napkin when her phone buzzed. She glanced at the screen, then swiped. "Denise. Hi."

"Hi! Where are you? We're waiting for you!"

Jenny blinked. "For what?"

"We're meeting for brunch today. Don't tell me you forgot!"

"I...what?"

"Our *Gen X Moms* brunch at the Harpoon? Didn't you read the group texts?"

It took Jenny a moment to catch on. "I left the group chat months ago, Denise. We haven't talked in weeks." She inhaled slowly. "You picked the Harpoon?"

"Sure! They have the best buffet. That's why we're here. Waiting for you."

Jenny crumpled the napkin into a small ball in her fist. "Denise, brunch in the *Harpoon*?"

"Uh...Oh! Oh. Because of—right. I thought maybe you had gotten past that block."

Block? Jenny swallowed. "I can't even walk past it."

"You poor thing. Of *course*. I understand." Denise's voice dropped to a conspiratorial whisper. "I mean, you could have let us *know* you're not coming. But I get it. I totally get it."

Jenny opened her fingers. The napkin fell on her plate with a soft thud. "Thanks."

"Hang on. The girls want to know about next month. We can go to a different hotel."

"I'm sorry, I won't be able to come. In fact, I don't know when I can come again."

"What? Why? You're not mad because of today, are you? The Harpoon Hotel *does* have the best buffet, Jenny. Unless—is it because of money?"

"I'm in California, Denise," Jenny said. She wasn't going to go into the gory details. "I'm traveling, and I don't know when I'll be back."

No, she's traveling in California, Jenny heard Denise hiss, the sound muffled as if Denise was pressing the phone into her sweater. Then, "That's great," Denise said, her voice clear again. "Take your mind off things, right?"

"Exactly." The waitress brought the check. Jenny tipped and smiled a thank-you.

"You'll get through this. You're strong," Denise said primly. "We Gen Xers are known to be tough."

"Sure," Jenny replied. "I suppose so."

"It'll all turn out great."

"Mm-hmm." It sounded different coming from Denise than from Glenn.

"It wasn't your fault. Don't think it was your fault."

Jenny exhaled, exasperated. "Denise, no offense...but how would you know that?"

"Well—you didn't do it, right?"

"By *doing it*, you mean *kill Stan*?"

There was a short pause. Then Denise whispered, "You *didn't*, did you?"

The burger and fries felt like chunks of cold metal in Jenny's stomach. She'd never been tight with the group of neighborhood women in the club, but she didn't realize how little they had in common. Did Denise seriously think Jenny was capable of doing something so horrible?

"Did you?" Denise was breathless.

Jenny bit her tongue, letting the sharp pain bring her back into focus and rein in the anger stirring in her chest. She stood and grabbed her purse. "I don't know, Denise."

Another pause. "You don't know in a *literal* sense? Or figuratively?" Still whispering.

"I have to go. Bye, Denise. Sorry I forgot to cancel and made you wait. Tell the others, okay?"

Jenny ended the call and stepped outside.

She never *insisted* they go to Acadia instead of Aspen. She hadn't insisted they buy a smaller house or fewer leather chairs at a thousand dollars a pop. She hadn't insisted on anything except that the kids could have pets and pick their college. Stan had demanded they go to his own Alma Mater. Jenny had talked him down and paid the kids' tuition with the money left from her inheritance.

Maybe if she'd had a job and paid for more things, if she had told Stan she wanted to stay home in the summer and swim in the sea, he would have been okay.

And maybe not.

The questions were pointless. Trying to think them up, as if they were hiding deep in her brain or her soul, was only driving her crazy because there were no answers.

Now, there was only the old family hotel.

Hopefully, it had power and water.

The sun was bright in the parking lot. Jenny pulled her sunglasses from her purse and put them on, thinking that she should get a sun hat, too.

She got back into the car and drove on. Vineyard after vineyard appeared as the small Toyota climbed the coastal mountain range. The hills grew more oaks, then cedars with wide, sprawling canopies. At the highest points, Jenny stopped at another vista point with breathtaking views and snapped a second selfie for the kids. She would text them before going to bed so she had something to look forward to.

Her stomach fluttered with anticipation as the street gradually shifted downward, because on the other side of the mountains was the coast.

CHAPTER 5

The sun was at its zenith by the time Jenny spotted the first redwood tree. This side of the mountain range was abruptly different from the dry ascent on the east. Someone had waved a magic wand, and suddenly the air was still and the light golden-green. Majestic tree trunks towered beside the road, their branches reaching for the sky. This was a new world, and the deeper the road led Jenny into it, the more her worries fell behind.

Jenny had loved Maine, but it was an adult love full of thoughts and comparisons. She had been grateful for the privilege of living on the Atlantic coast. It was beautiful, even more so because it reminded her of home.

But California was home.

It lived in the structure of her bones, the beating of her heart, and the shape of her senses. It was the glint of her gold anklet in cold blue water, the scent of morning fog in a cypress, the fiery sundown over the sea. It was returning home for a family dinner, sunburnt and salty-haired after an endless summer day of beachcombing with friends.

Of course, it would be different without Grandma Rosie and Mom and guests staying in the hotel.

Jenny's friends from back then, Ava, Faye, and Billie, would have married and moved away themselves. Jobs were few and far between in the small town.

Down the mountain went the car, and the green twilight brightened until the car left the forest, the giant sequoias staying behind like grizzled mountain guards.

Finally, there was the first glimpse of the sea. A soft sound escaped Jenny's throat, and she reached her hand out of the open window as if she could scoop up the view.

Often, fog rose where the cold water met the warm land. But today it was sunny, and the Pacific Ocean glittered in mesmerizing shades of blue.

"Look!" Jenny suddenly said out loud. "Pelicans!" She pointed at the birds flying in formation over the coastline, even though there was no one to look. "Pelicans," she whispered again. If only Audrey could see them.

Half an hour later, Jenny drove onto the bluff and into the small town of Mendocino Cove.

She passed the first handful of small white cottages. Their rickety fences were overgrown with blushing roses, velvety daylilies, and old, blooming rhododendrons in every shade of white, pink, and purple.

Jenny pulled to the curb and parked in front of a short row of quaint stores. On the other side of the empty street were meadows of wildflowers. Interspersed with sandy paths, the flowers stretched across the bluff all the way to the shimmering, glistening sea.

The air was warm and fragrant and welcoming, and Jenny opened her car door.

Her sneaker met the sandy street with a familiar crunch.

And just like that, she was back home.

"Hey—careful, there." A middle-aged man grinned at Jenny as he swerved out of her way. He was walking on the street instead of the sidewalk, tan and dressed in a T-shirt and shorts, sandals and a faded ball cap. Under his arm was a rolled-up beach towel, and the tote on his shoulder was clearly stuffed full of books. Jenny could see their sharp corners poking the canvas fabric.

"I'm sorry. I didn't see you." Jenny closed her car door and stepped aside to let him pass.

"I just came out of the Mermaid Galley. Best food in town, if you ask me." He stopped and smiled. "Just got here?"

She smiled back. He looked faintly familiar. But maybe that was her imagination playing tricks. "How can you tell?"

He pushed his cap back. "I don't remember seeing you around. Is it your first time in Mendocino Cove?"

"I grew up here, actually. I just got back from the East Coast."

"Ah, well done." The man nodded and resumed his walk, passing her on his way to the beach. "Welcome home," he called over his shoulder. "All the kids are moving to the city for jobs. We need everyone we can get."

She waved and watched him walk toward the wooden stairs that led down to the beach. Then she got her purse from the car and scanned the row of cute shops. There was a small jeweler, a boutique, a bookstore, and finally, the Mermaid Galley.

The place had already been there when she was a kid, but it used to have a different name and be more of a café, with only two or three heartier dishes.

There was only a sprinkle of patrons eating when Jenny went inside and asked the waitress for a table on the airy upper level. Mom had taken her here for a treat or special occasions to eat clam chowder. Jenny didn't have much money to spend on restaurants, but returning home was a special enough occasion to justify a tiny splurge.

"Hey, welcome to the Galley. My name is Hannah. What can I get you?" The waitress was in her early twenties and had laughing blue eyes, neat dreadlocks that were tied back into a ponytail of sorts, and a nose ring.

"Orange juice, please. Do you still have breakfast foods?" On an impulse, Jenny decided that this was the real start of her day.

"We do. Are you a bit hungry or a lot?"

Jenny smiled. It was hard not to when looking into those eyes. "In between."

Hannah nodded and pulled a menu from the pocket of her half apron. "We have French toast made with homemade challah bread, butter brioche with melted cheese, and avocado toast with a sunny side egg and feta cheese. There might also be an acai bowl left. It comes with fresh fruit and roasted walnuts, but I'd have to check. And if you want something more substantial, the breakfast burrito with scrambled eggs and salsa is a classic."

"It all sounds so good." On cue, Jenny's stomach grumbled. Suddenly, she was starving and weighing which option might be the most food for the money.

Looking thoughtful, Hannah tapped her notepad with a pencil. "Are you sure you're not ready for lunch? The portions are much bigger. How about battered fish that's fresh from the boat, served with fried vegetables and the best fries in town? The cook just finished making it. It'll be piping hot and super quick."

The breakfast plan went out of the window as quickly as it had come to her. Now that Hannah had mentioned fish, Jenny couldn't imagine ordering anything else. "Yes, please. And iced tea instead of orange juice, if you don't mind."

"You sound like you're from around here. But I haven't seen you before." Hannah scribbled a quick note and picked up the menu. "Where are you from?"

"Actually, I grew up in Mendocino Cove." From the corner of her eye, Jenny caught a movement. The woman at the table by the window had turned to look in her direction.

"Did you really?"

"My grandmother ran the hotel on the corner of Beach Street and Forgotten Lane." Jenny pushed her chair back a smidge to see the woman at the window.

The woman didn't look again. Maybe her back stiffened a little, as if she was listening in. Or maybe it was a trick of the light.

"The hotel at Beach and Forgotten? Is that still there?" Hannah asked, looking surprised.

Jenny opened her eyes wide. "I hope so! I'm planning on staying there. It didn't burn down or something, did it?"

Hannah chuckled. "Not that I know. I've not been to the beach in the Forgotten Cove for...oh goodness. Years."

Jenny nodded. "There's a reason it's called the Forgotten Cove. My mom used to say we'd be rich if we'd get a penny every time someone meant to come visit and forgot."

"It's so pretty over there, though." Hannah tucked the pencil back behind her ear. "Enough out of the way to be a little lonely. Are you going to stick around for a while? What's your name?"

"I'm Jenny. I guess I'll stay until I sort out a few things."

"Nice to meet you, Jenny. Do you still have people in town? Any family?"

"No family, at least." Jenny shrugged. "As for friends, I don't know. I've fallen out of touch, unfortunately."

Hannah retrieved her pencil, scribbled something on her pad, ripped off the page, and handed it to Jenny. "Here's my number. I live close by. Let me know if you need anything."

"Oh." Jenny took the page. "Gosh. Thank you." People in Portland were certainly friendly, but no one in

Jenny's circle would give their phone number to a complete stranger.

"Sure." Hannah nodded. "I'll be back with your food in a moment."

"Thank you. Thanks." Jenny watched Hannah leave but quickly looked away when Hannah started talking to the cook and she saw him looking in her direction.

When she turned back to the window, the woman who'd been listening was gone. Hannah brought her iced tea with lemon, and Jenny relaxed into her chair and took a sip while she admired the view of the Pacific Ocean.

It had already been a long day. But now that she was here, Jenny was ready for more.

"Told you it would be quick." Hannah reappeared and set a huge platter in front of Jenny, followed by a champagne flute full almost to the brim.

She looked at it. "Hannah, I'm afraid I didn't order champagne," she said quietly. Had she fallen back into her brunch habit and ordered more than her new budget allowed?

"It's prosecco, and it's on the house." Hannah smiled. "Welcome home, Jenny."

"Goodness. Thank you, Hannah."

"Thank him," Hannah said and pointed. Jenny looked up and saw the cook, kitchen towel slung over his shoulder, wink at her. Then he lifted his own matching glass of prosecco to cheer.

It made Jenny laugh. She waved and raised her glass back to him.

Jenny ate her fish and chips, which were as promised piping hot and delicious, drank her iced tea and celebratory prosecco, and wondered why she couldn't forget the woman who had glanced over.

When she was done, she paid, learned that the cook's name was Michael, promised Hannah she'd be back soon, and left.

The last few minutes of her journey back home were achingly familiar. The road led through a riot of California poppies, lavender irises, and pink lupines. Soon, Jenny left the mansion and the bluff, and then she flicked the blinker to turn off Main onto Forgotten. She pulled up in front of her old home, parked under the old cedar tree, and got out.

The hotel rose at the corner of Beach and Forgotten, overlooking the beach in the small cove. Far from having burned down, the house looked like an old lady sitting in the sun. It lazily blinked its many windows at the sea.

"Hello again," she whispered and shaded her eyes against the bright sun. "I'm back."

A line of pelicans swerved off course. A sea lion barked on the beach, and waves crashed against the rocks in a well-practiced, everlasting dance. Otherwise, all was quiet. Gripping the old bearded key she'd kept in her pocket throughout the trip, Jenny walked to the door.

CHAPTER 6

G uess what." Faye brushed her wavy hair out of her face. It was getting too long for the beach, and the sun had bleached the hazel color into the undetermined battle ground that lay between blond and brown. She propped her knees up and relaxed her back against the warm wood of the driftwood log.

"I'm guessing you had eggs for breakfast." Billie crossed her arms and squinted at the water.

Faye shifted to lay her head on her friend's shoulder. "You look like a mad pirate waiting for her schooner when you frown like that. Guess again."

"Just tell me already. Not all of us have your crystal ball energy."

"You have enough." Faye picked up a small shell and crumbled off the fragile rim. "I actually did eat eggs."

"Well done," Billie said. "I had pancakes with raspberry jam. And chicken salad for lunch."

"I went to eat at the Mermaid Galley for lunch. I sat upstairs so I could watch the hummingbirds."

"Did Hannah fill the sugar feeders?"

Faye tossed her head. "She said she did, but I'm not so sure. It was only noon, and they were already empty—how much sugar water can they drink in one go?"

"A thimble full per bird?"

"A thimble? You can fit the entire bird into a thimble. Beaks, wings, stiff little legs and all."

"So they drink less than a thimble." Billie sighed.

"Hannah claims the hummingbirds are getting worse every day, and she's getting fed up with them. They chase each other."

"Total thugs."

"If you ask me, Hannah just forgets to fill the feeders. It's no wonder the hummingbirds are getting restless."

"Pshaw, those terrible millennials. Only one job and can't even do it right." Billie groaned. "Move over, kiddo. My bum's starting to hurt. If fifty is the new twenty, my body sure didn't get the email."

Faye moved over, and Billie rearranged herself in the sand and leaned back against the sun-soaked log. Then she folded her fingers behind her head, closed her eyes, and held her face into the sun. "We could fill the feeders ourselves. We'll just ask Hannah to slip us a key to the restaurant."

"Michael will be happy to hear we'll be traipsing in and out of his restaurant at will to feed the birds." Faye giggled.

Michael was a good man and an even better cook, but the Galley was his kingdom and he was her tyrant. Before Hannah arrived to swing her dreadlocks rebelliously at Michael, his staff had lasted about as long as a hummingbird in a stiff sea breeze.

"That is true." Billie opened one lazy eye to look at Faye. "What were we talking about before we went off on the sugar water tangent?"

Faye moistened her lips. "I want to tell you about the woman who came to eat."

"A tourist? Someone Michael has his eye on? It's been a while since his last fling. He's probably getting bored."

A small boy screamed as an icy wave licked up his leg, and his sister collapsed laughing on the warm sand. Faye smiled at them.

"Hey, focus, you. Who was it? Who was the mystery woman in the Mermaid Galley?" Billie asked impatiently.

"I think it was Jenny. Our Jenny."

"Jenny...Summers?" Billie's arms sank to her sides. "Jenny Summers?"

"I think so. I think it was her." Faye nodded.

For a long while, Billie was silent. "Are you sure? Why would she visit after all these years? She didn't even come back when her grandmother died. The entire county came. Everyone but Jenny."

"I don't know why she didn't come back then," Faye said reasonably. "A thousand reasons could have kept her."

"Her grandmother's spirit will never rest because of it."

"Don't say that. You don't even believe in spirits. I'm the one who does. And I think Rosie's spirit is just fine."

"It's probably haunting the cove."

"Doing what? Diving for abalone and scaring the sea lions?"

"Maybe it wasn't Jenny." Billie lifted her legs and brushed the sand off the rolled-up hem of her jeans. "None of us look like we did back in the day."

Faye arched her eyebrows. "I beg to differ. I look exactly like I did back in the day, and you do too."

Billie laughed. "We have wrinkles from staring at the sea too long."

"Our aura hasn't changed," Faye declared.

"Aura fiddlesticks, my dear. Wrinkles and gray hairs—that's what people see. Did you get a good look at Jenny?"

"I didn't want to stare."

"Ah. So it's more one of your purple feelings?"

"Leave my purple feelings be, Billie." Faye shot her friend a warning glance.

Billie shrugged and shoved the sleeves of her faded gray T-shirt over her tanned shoulders to avoid a tan line. "Then why do you think it was her?"

"I heard her talk about the hotel at Beach and For-gotten. She asked Hannah if it was still standing."

Billie dropped her head, staring at the sand. "The hotel at Beach and Forgotten? I've not been to the cove in years."

"Me neither. I just keep...forgetting." Faye smiled. "I'm telling you, there's a charm protecting that little cove."

"It's more mundane than that, Faye. It's called For-gotten Lane because the turn off the main road is completely hidden in vines and bushes and nobody can ever find the darn thing. You're past before you know it, and then people just go to the next beach instead of turning back."

"We used to find it just fine when Jenny lived there," Faye pointed out. "We forever hung out in the cove, remember?"

Billie hooked her arms around her knees and nodded.

"Well, how about we just go over and knock on the door of the hotel?" Faye asked gently. "If it's not Jenny, I sure would like to know who's living there now."

Billie looked back. "Did she look like Jenny at all?"

"She had blond hair."

Billie sighed, and then she stood. "Let's go and see. If it's not Jenny, whoever it is probably shouldn't be there."

Happy to have recruited her friend, Faye went to wash the sand off her feet in the clear water.

The kids were still running up and down the beach, screaming and laughing and throwing clumps of sandy algae. Their parents sat on a blanket at a safe distance, arms around each other's shoulders. A dog as big as a calf and with hair like a mop sat beside them, his head swiveling between the kids. Faye watched for a moment.

When the little girl went past her ankles into the water, the dog jumped up and barked. "Get back, Mimi!" the dad yelled. "Don't get your shorts wet!"

Little Mimi threw her head back in protest, but when the dog ran to her, she started laughing. Arm around the pet's neck, she squealed happily as he dragged her to sand and safety.

"I wish I had a dog like that." Back at the log, Faye toweled off her feet, knowing there was no way to keep the sand out of beach shoes.

"You're not a dog person," Billie said.

"And you're being irritating."

"No, I'm not. You're just not a dog person. And you already have a cat."

"Tantor is not my cat. He barely even is a cat."

"Think Jenny wants to see us?" Billie asked. "What if it's just memories and nostalgia?"

"Then we can build a new friendship."

"Nostalgia is like shifting sand—not exactly a stable base for building things."

"Billie, it's not just childhood nostalgia. We had something real. Maybe our sisterhood has frayed around the edges, but it has a solid core." Faye smiled and spread her hands in a question. "Why else would she come back?"

"There are a thousand other reasons, Faye." Billie shook the sand off her sandals and hitched her sun-bleached beach tote over her shoulder. "Let's go and find out."

CHAPTER 7

Jenny's old key was stuck in the lock of the hotel's ornate double doors.

Wiggling didn't work. Nor did swearing under her breath.

If Auntie Georgie had really hired someone to come and make sure everything was all right, they used another door.

Jenny stood on tiptoes. She cupped her hands against the stained glass and peeked into the oval window by the door. Yep—there was the grand foyer. Large, empty, and dimly lit.

She dropped back on her heels and returned to her key. "Can you please let me *in?*" Frustrated, she hammered a fist against the door. Then she took a deep breath and tried the key again.

It didn't turn.

"The only way is forward," Jenny warned the hotel. She took a step back to figure out what the way forward was. Raw force?

Raw force.

Jenny went back to the car to grab her cashmere sweater from the passenger seat and her duffle bag from the trunk. Mostly to let the hotel know she meant business. She was going to get inside. If it took breaking a window, she'd break a window.

Walking back to the double doors, Jenny glanced at the row of upstairs windows. Had something moved in the left one? She squinted. Nothing there—it must have been a trick of the light.

"Door, you get one more chance. After that I'll smash a window, and I'll start with one that has stained glass. You've been warned." She put the bag down, wrapped a sleeve around the ornate bow of the key, and firmly grabbed the soft fabric with both hands. "Bend, but don't break," she ordered, repeating one of Grandma Rosie's pieces of well-worn advice, and leaned in.

With the sound of a seal crying out in the fog, the key turned a little. "All right!" Jenny's heart fluttered like a monarch on milkweed. She leaned in again, pressing on the key again. Something in the lock gave way—maybe a rust deposit. She let go. Then she took off the sweater and turned the key the rest of the way.

The lock clicked, and the door swung open.

"Thank you," Jenny whispered, relieved. She took her bag and stepped inside the old hotel.

By now, it was properly hot outside. Jenny had been grateful for the shade of the old cypress while she wrestled with the door, but she had still broken into a sweat. But here, inside the grand foyer, it was cool. Except for the small oval one by the door, the windows were covered with white drop cloths. The filtered sunlight cast a mysterious twilight on the tiled mosaic floor, the high ceilings with their intricate crown molding, and the sweeping staircase with its rich, polished wood banister that spiraled gracefully upward.

"Welcome home, myself." Jenny put down her bag beside the entrance and closed the door. The wood creaked like a pirate ship. Or maybe an old captain clearing his throat.

She couldn't remember any creaking. Maybe the boards had warped. Or maybe the creaking had always been there but was covered by all the other noises and sounds that had filled the hotel. Jenny put her head in her neck to inspect the ceiling. A creaking floor was not a problem, but falling crown molding would be.

The chandelier above her was made of hundreds of translucent blue and green pieces of sea glass, each one as unique as the woman who'd collected it. Over years and generations, the glass filled a large floor vase. For Rosie's fiftieth birthday, Grandpa had replaced the sea glass with decoy marbles and, in a fabled act of bravery, snuck the glass out of the house. Over weeks of stolen evenings, he soldered the glass into a beautiful, multi-tiered chandelier.

Grandma had loved the chandelier so much she almost forgave Grandpa for emptying the vase.

Jenny walked to the check-in counter and set her sweater on it. Then she flipped the light switch. A myriad of soft blue and green shades dappled the room, making it look peaceful and serene. Jenny went into the small restroom and tried the vintage brass faucet at the sink. Water rushed into the white basin, running hot after a moment. Jenny let out a breath of relief. Georgie had followed through on her promise.

However unreliable her aunt was—now and then, she did come through.

Jenny wandered into the kitchen. Here, too, everything was like she remembered. The gleam of the copper pots and pans hanging from the ceiling rack was dulled by dust and disuse, but the double-wide butcher block island was brightly lit by the skylight above. There was still the same enormous custom-built cooking range, its cast-iron and brass construction standing proudly against a brick wall. It was large enough for several cooks to work side-by-side and still stay friends. Walking by, Jenny trailed her fingers over a long wooden table. Even though there was a formal dining room, the family and their guests had often eaten in the kitchen.

The hotel was glamorous, but its manager had been eminently practical. Their guests rarely had money to spare; sometimes they couldn't even pay for their room. But Grandma took in anyone for the asking.

How she made it work, Jenny had no idea. As a kid, she'd been busy with school and swimming and playing with her friends, and neither Mom nor Georgie nor Grandma ever talked about money. They weren't rich, but there was always good food, neat clothes, and pocket money for ice creams.

Mom, Georgie, and Grandma had been the fixtures of her young life. Hotel guests came and went like waves on the ocean. There were single men and women traveling alone, a few families on vacation. Young, middle-aged, old. Often, the women were pregnant or had small kids. On a few occasions, there was much excitement and running, and later there were dinner stories of last-minute car rides to the hospital.

Jenny had only later understood that her grandmother was taking in women who had nowhere else to go. From bits and pieces of conversation that hummed to a stop when she entered the room, Jenny pieced together that Rosie had made sure babies born out of wedlock were delivered safely and mothers were able to recover from giving birth before heading back out into the world.

When the women returned with unsure smiles and their hospital-blanket-swaddled babies in their arms, Rosie would welcome them with a festive beach bonfire. The family and all their guests gathered to roast foil potatoes and fish and scallops and corn grilled on sticks.

Mom would bring out her coconut cake and Georgie the yellow booties she had knitted, and everyone applauded when they were presented to the new mother. They shared the cake and put the booties on the baby and took photos of the party with flashlight cubes like shooting stars on the beach.

Jenny also had a pair of yellow booties so small they fit her thumb. Maybe she had been the first baby to be welcomed back with a beach bonfire. Maybe, she sometimes thought, she had been the reason there had been so many of these celebrations at the hotel.

Someone always knew how to play a guitar or a ukulele or blow a tune on a harmonica, and one time, a guest had brought an accordion. Jenny would dance to the music under the stars, and the young mother would laugh and sing and only sometimes peer into the folds of the bundle in her arms with worry in her moonlit eyes.

CHAPTER 8

J enny picked a stoneware custard cup from one of
the hutches that displayed china and glass, racks of
piping bags and decorative molds, bowls and rolling
pins, and a dozen other tools. Grandma had insisted on
everything being sparkling clean at all times. But when
Jenny blew into the little cup, dust motes sailed into the
air like tiny brigs setting sail into the unknown.

She waved the motes away.

Jenny went to the sink and tried the faucet. She had
to force the handle and wait until it ran clear, then she
put a stopper into the sink and checked the cupboard
beneath. There was an array of plastic bottles of dish
soap. Had they been here for the last decade?

She squeezed the bottles over the sink one by one
until she found one that wasn't dried out. When the
sink was full of hot, sudsy water, she remembered the
closet in the butler's pantry where she found a pair of
Grandma's faded pink dishwashing gloves.

She laid them beside the sink.

Suddenly, she couldn't breathe. "Calm down," she
whispered to herself and hunched over to catch her
breath. She couldn't panic. She couldn't miss Grandma

so much it suffocated her. Or her childhood. Or Mom. Even the many guests she had loved with a child's sincere and straightforward love.

In the end, it wasn't self-discipline and willpower but a loud knock that widened her lungs again. Jenny straightened and gasped a few deep breaths, then listened.

What was that?

She went to the living room and stood in the door, taking a moment to look around.

It was a law of nature that when you returned to your childhood home after a long time, everything must look smaller.

But not the living room. It looked even more spacious than Jenny remembered.

A long time ago, Grandpa and his friends removed the wall between the drawing room and the grand parlor of the original mansion. There was a short-lived attempt to call the large new room the saloon. But people grew weary of sounding like cowboys, and when Grandma declared one night over roast potatoes and venison that it should just be called the living room from now on, everyone breathed a sigh of relief.

White, floor-to-ceiling French doors opened onto the patio and the beach, and Grandma kept ferns and palms in terracotta pots inside and out. The blue ocean, tamed by the cliffs hugging the Forgotten Cove, provided a spectacular, sparkling background.

Jenny could see the hotel guests now, sitting in the armchairs and sofas and white wicker chairs, wearing shorts and sundresses, talking, laughing, sipping iced lemonade, eating coconut cake, and watching the kids and babies play.

It was so tempting an image that she sat in one of the chairs herself instead of going back to the kitchen to wash the custard cups. The bang had probably just been a bird hitting a window or maybe the water boiler heating up.

Jenny leaned her head back, wishing she had a slice of her mother's coconut cake.

The hotel had been one of the first Victorian mansions in the county. It had belonged to wealthy lumberyard owner Oscar Morris, who had set his mind on building his widowed mother, Gladys, the biggest, most beautiful house on the West Coast.

To his dismay, his mother lived in the vast mansion for only six months. Then she declared herself tired of dusting ten bedrooms and keeping a horse and buggy just so she could visit her friends. Undaunted by her son's tantrum, Gladys moved in with a friend who had a small, cheerful cottage in the village and a spare room. There, they played canasta into the night, tended to the roses in the front yard while letting the backyard grow into a merry mess of weeds and wildflowers, and walked the small distance to the shops and their friends' cottages whenever they felt like it.

Busy with politics and trees and saws, forming unions and raising a young family while running for mayor, Oscar soon sold his big mansion in the little cove. The town eventually named the two small, unpaved roads—one going down toward the water, one running the width of the cove—so the mailman could find the house.

Eager to spoil his bride, Grandpa set to work fixing it up. He broke down walls and added windows and shelves, plumbing pipes and brass faucets, and claw-footed bathtubs where they weren't already until Grandma was able to put up everyone and their dog in style. He finished the last bay window a week to the day before peacefully and forever falling asleep on his carpentry blueprint for a bigger, better hutch to house his wife's collection of flea market china.

Jenny stood and went to draw back the long, white curtains hiding the French doors. Bright sunlight flooded the room. Behind the glass and a few patio stones sprawled the golden beach of the cove that sloped down to the Pacific.

"Whoa," Jenny whispered.

She had forgotten how it felt to live on a beach. On a fine day, you simply threw open the doors and stepped into the sand. And in Mendocino Cove, every day was a fine day.

A long line of pelicans flew low over the water. Somewhere, a sea lion barked.

Another knocking sound startled her out of her reverie.

"For crying out loud. Someone's at the *front* door," Jenny murmured and went back to the foyer, passing the enormous fireplace with its twin cast-iron peacock screens, the plush sofas and armchairs, and the dusty grand piano that didn't fit through any of the hotel doors and never held a tune. Maybe it was the maintenance company checking in.

Jenny took a moment to brush the dust off her T-shirt, tuck her hair behind her ears, and fix her polite smile on her lips.

A quick glance into the gilded mirror to her left showed that she looked travel-worn but collected. She opened the door.

CHAPTER 9

The door opened, and a figure appeared in the dim, green-and-blue-speckled light of the foyer like a ghost from the past.

Billie blinked, trying to fit her memories to the sight in front of her. The features were both familiar and not. The hair was still dirty blond and the eyes the same blue that had promised her friendship forever. But the eyelids were heavier, and their expression guarded. The first crow's feet scratched their corners, and the formerly round cheeks were hollow and high-boned.

Whatever small changes there were—the woman before her was clearly Jenny Summers.

"Can I help?" Jenny smiled politely.

"Hi, Jenny," Faye said, her voice breathlessly dropping the last letter. "It's us."

"Faye?" Jenny stepped out into the sunshine. "And *Billie?*"

"Hi, Jenny." Billie's throat felt tight. "How are you? What are you doing here?"

"I came back home. At least for a while," Jenny replied after a small eternity. She wrapped her arms around herself even though it was hot. "I didn't think you two were still in Mendocino Cove."

Because you never asked, Billie wanted to say. But it was a knee-jerk reaction, and she was glad the words didn't slip out. Now that Jenny stood in front of them, Billie didn't know *what* she wanted to say.

Faye inhaled. "Lots of people moved. Kerry lives in Arizona, and Ava married someone in Seattle."

"I didn't know. I lost track."

"Hmm," Billie hummed, just to contribute something. It would have been easy enough to stay in touch. But her picture of Jenny as a lady who lunched, unconcerned about the death of the grandmother who'd raised her, had already crumbled.

"I missed you, Jen," Faye said shyly, interrupting Billie's thoughts. "I was sorry when we fell out of touch."

"Oh. Oh." Jenny dropped her arms by her side as if she'd held a heavy weight and suddenly dropped it.

"Are you okay?" Billie took half a step back. She wasn't ready to deal with more emotions than already churned in her stomach.

"Yes." Jenny cleared her throat, twice. "I didn't expect to see you."

"Is it good or bad that you do? See us, I mean?" Faye asked after another pause.

"It's the best." Jenny's lips quivered for a moment, but then she pressed them into a tight line. "I missed both of you. I missed you so much."

And then Jenny lost control and burst into tears.

A day ago, Billie would have rolled her eyes. How much could Jenny miss them when she never texted, let alone visited? But now... Those tears were real. Big and fat and wet, they were without pretense. They left pitiful tracks on Jenny's hollow cheeks and ran down her nose and chin where they hung before dripping on her shirt, the jeans, the ground.

"Well." Stumped, Billie looked at Faye, who helplessly shrugged back. "Uh. Don't cry, Jenny."

"Yeah, Jen. Don't cry," Faye said helpfully. "We're right here."

Jenny pressed her palms to her eyes, stemming the flow. "I'm sorry. I'm okay. It's been a really long day." Awkwardly, she dried her face with her shirt and the inside of her wrist.

Holding Billie's gaze, Faye nodded at Jenny.

What? What do you want me to do? Billie mentally asked Faye, but Faye unfortunately didn't mentally hear it. Still holding her gaze, she nodded again.

"*What?*" Billie whispered.

Faye rolled her eyes and turned back to Jenny.

"Um. Can I give you a hug?" Faye opened her arms tentatively.

"Yes. Yes, please, Faye." Jenny's eyes shimmered again, but at least now she was smiling. Without further ado, she stepped out and embraced Faye.

It wasn't the polite kiss-the-air hug Billie half expected. It was a good old Jenny hug that stuck to the ribs and made you feel safe and whole for an hour afterward.

"Welcome back," Faye whispered into Jenny's hair and stepped back.

Okay. If Faye wanted to hug Jenny, that was her—

"Billie? Can I give you a hug too?" Now it was Jenny who tentatively opened her arms.

"Uh, I'm good. I'm no more of a hugger than I was back then." Billie narrowed her eyes. Jenny's smile was *widening.* And her arms didn't drop even though Billie had clearly—

"Billie!" Faye snapped. "Give Jenny a hug! She's *just* come back."

Billie threw up her chin. "Oh fine! Go ahead."

With a sound that was half sob, half laugh, Jenny threw her arms around Billie's neck and pulled her close.

Just as Billie remembered, it was a hug that stuck to the ribs. She couldn't help but lift her arms and hug Jenny back.

"Thanks, Billie." Jenny gave her a last good squish and let go.

Apparently, hugging Faye made Jenny cry, and hugging Billie made her laugh.

"You don't deserve hugs," Billie growled and crossed her hands behind her back. "You never wrote back after my last email."

"Oh for goodness' sake with that email," Faye muttered.

"She *didn't*!" Why would no one acknowledge that it was rude not to answer?

Faye shook her hazel curls. When Faye shook her hair like that, things were about to get messy.

"She didn't," Billie murmured rebelliously but not very loud.

"I'm sorry I didn't, Bills. I really am. I know I was a crap friend, but there was a lot going on."

Billie bit her lip. She was forty-five and had to stop her lips from quivering like a little girl who'd been pushed on the playground. "Okay. It's fine."

Jenny went back inside, opening the door wide. "Any chance you'll come in? I promise I won't cry anymore. I'm dying to catch up."

"I'd love to catch up too." Faye hooked her arm firmly under Billie's. "It's been so long. I barely know who you are anymore."

A shadow darkened Jenny's face. "I'm not sure I can tell you, Faye."

There was something forlorn in the downcast eyes and the drop of her shoulders. The lump in Billie's throat, already softened by the hug, now melted like salt in water. "Sure, Jenny, we can visit for a while." Freeing her arm from Faye's, Billie walked straight past Jenny into the old hotel.

"Yeah, let's visit." Faye followed.

The door closed with a soft thud that had lived in Billie's memories without her knowledge. How often had she heard that sound?

She stopped because she couldn't very well lead the way as if they were still ten years old.

"Um." Jenny kneaded her fingers. "I'm afraid I only just arrived a few minutes ago." She nodded at the duffle bag on the floor. "I haven't got much to offer in the way of drinks. Or food. Only some airplane crackers."

"No worries." Faye opened her purse and pulled out a chocolate bar. "We have this, baby."

"Yeah." Billie fished the unopened bottle of lemon seltzer from her tote bag. "Chocolate, crackers, and fizzy drinks. It's a picnic."

Jenny gave them an uncertain smile. It was so unlike her that Billie lowered her bottle. "Hey, are you okay?"

"Yeah. Yeah. To make a picnic out of a chocolate bar and water is just so...sweet. It's so sweet of you to do this."

"Not very." Faye marched past Jenny into the living room. "You know, Jen, I haven't stopped by the cove for years. But the moment you arrive, I rush over here! Is that weird or what? I always wonder..." Her voice trailed off. "Forget it, I'm just rambling. It's good to be back here."

"Me too. Should we go find glasses?" Jenny pointed a thumb over her shoulder.

"Yep." Billie gestured for Jenny to go first. "Let's use fancy glasses and cut up the snickers bar, then put the slices on crackers. How does that sound?"

Jenny started toward the kitchen. "Honestly, a thin slice of snickers on a cracker sounds pretty good."

"I agree." Billie smiled. "Let's eat outside, like in the olden times."

Jenny smiled back. Not the small adult smile from when she opened the door, but the old one from way back when they were kids.

But there was a story to the adult smile. And Billie was here to find out about it.

CHAPTER 10

O ne thing I never noticed as a kid"—Faye picked up one of the pillows that crowded the sofas in the living room and studied the embroidered rose on it—"is that Rosie had such a Victorian taste." When Faye thought of Jenny's Grandma, she saw images of the old woman smoking her little clay pipe by a beach bonfire and putting up women in need. Cooking in the kitchen came to mind too, and harvesting mussels from the cliffs that hugged the cove.

Billie took the pillow from her and squinted critically at the swirling petals. "I didn't notice either. I guess kids just take it as it comes."

"Look at that." Faye went to the wall behind the piano and peered at a row of neatly stitched sayings in heavy wood frames. "Did Rosie make these herself, Jenny?"

"Yes, as well as the pillows. Her mother taught her how to do it. Grandma tried to teach me too." Jenny smiled. "Funny. I haven't thought about that for ages."

"Aww, I remember Rosie embroidering." Billie plopped on the sofa. "What do they say?"

Jenny's smile reached her eyes. "They're Grandma's favorite sayings. You know how she had these corny sayings, like a cliché, but with a twist of her own?"

Billie laughed. "Do I? X always marks the spot. Better late than never, but earlier is best."

"Exactly."

"It took me a while to figure out the real phrasings," Billie said. "Pretty sure insisting I had them right caused at least one breakup with a boyfriend."

Faye took off a frame and read, "Don't count your chickens before they hatch, but do count your eggs." She giggled and put it back. "Did you make any of these, Jenny? You said Rosie showed you how to do it."

"Honestly, I'm a lost cause when it comes to craft. I don't like it, and I can't do it. Especially if it's anything involving a needle and thread. Poor Grandma. She was so determined to teach me."

"No luck, huh?"

"Nope. I was as hopeless as she was talented." Jenny shook her head. "No matter how much she made me practice, my fingers would twist into a knot. I never managed a clean stitch."

Faye pointed to another frame. "That one here is very à propos. It says, What doesn't kill you can still leave a few bruises." She smiled. "That's what she said when I fell in the rock pool and cut my shin."

"Ah," Jenny said. "Right. I remember hearing that one a lot."

"This one shows the cove." Faye pointed at an especially large frame with a stitched scene of the beach and white-crested waves. "Look at all the colors! It's so pretty. I wonder if it's worth something."

"Faye has a secondhand store," Billie explained dryly. "She can't help but price everything for its resale value."

"Sorry." Faye smiled an apology at Jenny. "I'm embarrassed to say that Billie's right. Appraising things has become a habit."

"Oh, I see." Jenny nodded. "I have to see your store. I love secondhand stores. But I'm afraid nothing in this hotel is mine to sell; it all belongs to Aunt Georgie. And the embroideries remind me too much of Grandma to sell, anyway."

"Memories are invaluable," Faye agreed. She didn't point out that despite Billie's comment, she hadn't asked for the embroideries.

Jenny went to pull another curtain aside and crinkled her nose. "Do you smell that? Like cold pipe smoke. These curtains are musty."

"Really? Rosie's pipe?" Billie came to smell the sheer white fabric.

Faye wasn't done studying the frames. "One has a big cross on it," she remarked. "At least I think that's what it is." Unlike the others, it wasn't very good. The stitches wobbled drunkenly here and there as if they couldn't make up their mind, too thick in some places and too sparse in others.

"A religious cross?" Billie lopped the floral pillow into the air and caught it again.

"No, it's turned like the letter X."

Jenny suddenly laughed. "Oh, that actually is mine. I can't believe Grandma hung it up on the wall!" She tugged on a curtain that was stuck.

"Was it part of an alphabet?"

"No, it wasn't. It was... Whenever I got stuck, Grandma would chalk down a tiny cross on my fabric to show me where to put the next stitch and say, X always marks the spot. So for my pièce de résistance, I stitched her a big old X." Jenny yanked the stuck curtain open. "When it was done, I presented the X to her and declared I'd rather live in the cliff caves than thread one more needle."

Faye grinned. "What did Rosie say to that?"

"She said I had ten left fingers but an answer for everything." Jenny smiled. "I forgot that happened."

"It was sweet of Rosie to frame it and hang it next to her pretty cove."

"I definitely didn't deserve the honor," Jenny agreed.

Billie straightened the rest of the floral sofa pillows. Dust whirled, and she sneezed. "Can you open more doors, Jen?"

"Sure." Jenny grabbed the last curtain still covering the French doors and pulled it aside.

The room had already been flooded with light, but now that the last curtain was gone, sunlight filled every last corner of the room like a golden tide.

"I'd book a room if the hotel was still open! The light makes it easy to forget about the dusty pillows and musty curtains." Faye went to help throw wide door after door until the entire wall was open to the beach.

She held her face in the fresh sea breeze. The scent of salt and kelp was delicious after the stale air inside, and the screaming gulls and rushing waves harmonized in the sea's very own symphony.

Jenny kicked off her sneakers and stuffed her socks into them, then stepped out onto the patio. "Hot!" She danced across the sun-heated pavers and onto the beach, where she stopped to dig her toes into the fine sand. "Oooh." She closed her eyes and opened her arms wide. "The sand is perfect."

Billie held out her hand to Faye. "If you give me your chocolate bar, I'll put them on the crackers. I'm not sure when she ate last."

"I know." Jenny was too skinny for Faye's taste too. No, not skinny but gaunt. The way you looked when you worried and skipped meals because you didn't have an appetite. "We'll have to fatten her up a bit and get some color back in her cheeks." Faye handed over her snack. Then she got out of her sandals and followed Jenny.

"Ouch!" Faye hopped across the stones and into the sand, then joined Jenny where the sea met the land and crystal-clear waves cooled the sand. "That's better, hey?" She elbowed Jenny lightly and smiled.

"It's so much better." Jenny stood, looking at the horizon, the sea breeze playing with her hair. "Faye, you have no idea. This is what I needed. I don't think a day has passed in my life where I didn't miss this beach."

Carrying the plate with their humble snack, Billie joined them in time to catch Jenny's last words. "Why didn't you visit?" she asked, and Faye heard the sadness hidden in the words. "Why did you never come to see us?"

Jenny sighed. "I don't know. I asked Stan if we could take a trip, come for vacation."

"You asked him? Couldn't you tell him?"

"I should have." Jenny's shoulders dropped, and she looked down at the water washing over her feet. "There's a lot I should've done. I should have come alone without him."

Faye frowned. "I'm getting vibes."

"Major vibes." Jenny ran a hand through her hair. "I don't want to talk about it. I'll tell you if you want to know. But not now. Not yet."

Faye glanced at Billie. It didn't sound like their friend had a happy marriage.

Billie nodded back. "Jen, are you going to stay in Mendocino Cove for a while?" she asked lightly.

"A while," Jenny replied and finally tore her gaze away from the water. "I don't know how long."

"Let's sit and eat a cracker or two." Billie pointed at the rocks that sided the little cove. The rocks were sprinkled with patches of silvery dried salt and fresh tide pools. They were flat and easy to climb on, and there were plenty of good spots to sit. Only farther out did they turn into jagged cliffs.

"Sure." Jenny's eyes lit up as she surveyed their old favorite spots, and she started walking.

Faye's heart lifted too as she joined her friend. "Remember when I told you the story about the hook on the door handle?"

"No," Billie replied quickly.

But Jenny giggled. "We had to yell for my mom to come and walk us back into the house. You were too scared to go without her."

"I was eight." Billie tried her best to sound dignified.

Faye grinned and bumped Billie with her hip. "We were too, and it didn't bother us. Scaredy-cat."

"Hey! Stop doing that! I almost dropped the plate."

"We were eight years old and sleeping on the rocks by the sea," Jenny said. "Nowadays, they would probably call child protective services on our parents. But we had a good time."

"I know. Let's go and see whether our stone table is still there." Faye sloshed through the cold water, kicking washed-up kelp out of the way and picking up a lemon-yellow shell to show Jenny.

She didn't want her friend to think about the dangers of the wild beauty that surrounded them everywhere. Sooner or later, Jenny's thoughts would turn to the way all that wild beauty had swallowed up her mother. Maybe Jenny had come to terms with what happened. Maybe it was an open wound.

The wind lifted and tugged on Faye's hair like a person. A shiver trickled down her spine, and she glanced over her shoulder. For a moment, she thought she saw a mist, but when she blinked, it was gone.

Just a trick of the light.

It was a beautiful day with skies as blue as the sea was cold. The air was dry and fragrant with salt and the scent of cypress trees.

Nobody stood behind Faye, and no mist wavered in the air.

"Hey, Faye! Are you coming?" Billie called. "What are you doing?"

Faye shaded her eyes. "I thought I saw a conch shell."

Billie stopped. "Is it intact?"

"No. I was wrong." Faye dropped her hand. There was nothing. Yet her spine and her blood tingled as if a warm breath had tickled her neck. "I can't see anything at all."

"Then hurry up! The chocolate is melting in the sun, and things are turning into an awful mess."

"Coming." Faye started to run so she would catch up with her friends. She didn't stop until she, too, was climbing on rocks that felt smooth and warm and safe.

CHAPTER 11

They ate the crackers, getting chocolate smears on their cheeks and fingers and laughing about them. Finally, Jenny stood to wash off her sticky hands in a large tidepool. Something moved, catching her attention. She squatted down, keeping her shadow off the water. Slowly, a sea anemone unfurled from a small brown bump on the side of the rock into a bouquet of lavender and green tentacles. Shrimp dashed like ghosts across the bottom, and a beautiful red crab, the size of a dime, came out from a hiding spot under a barnacle-encrusted piece of wood to wave its claw at Jenny.

"Hello, little fellow," she whispered and waved back with a finger.

This lunch was about as different as it could be from the one in the Harpoon Hotel.

"Hey, Jenny, is it okay if we go back in?" Billie called. She was shaking the crumbs off her T-shirt. "I have to pee."

Faye picked up the plate and stood as well. "I'm getting too hot," she declared. "I didn't bring my hat."

"Sure." Jenny climbed over the rocks, avoiding the slippery patches of seaweed. Mom had often collected the edible algae, and Jenny tried to remember the names. Wakame and sugar kelp were good in broth. The brown or red algae with the flat, rubbery leaves that were covered in tiny knobs were called Turkish washcloth and Turkish towel. Grandma had sometimes used them as thickener when she ran out of cornstarch. Sea Lettuce made for a bright green salad. Sea balloons weren't edible, Jenny seemed to remember, but their squishy, olive-shaped bubbles on shaggy branches were a favorite hiding spot for crabs. Sometimes, Grandma had collected them for dinner too, making a delicious stew from mussels and crabs and the fish she bought in the harbor.

They reached the house, and Jenny sat on the step to rub the sand off her feet.

"You're getting a sunburn." Faye sat beside her. "Be careful."

Jenny looked at her pale winter arms. They were indeed flushed pink. "I suppose the May sun in Maine is one thing. The sun in Mendocino Cove is another."

"That's probably true." Billie let herself fall on the threshold too and started brushing her feet. "Is Maine nice?"

"Maine is beautiful," Jenny said. "Similar to Northern California in many respects, but also completely different."

"You have to tell me more about Maine sometime," Billie said. "I've always wanted to go, but there was never a good reason."

Jenny hugged her knees. "Visiting me would have been a good reason." Regret quieted her voice. "I wish we'd stayed in touch."

"Look at us, clean feet and all." Faye was done and went inside. "Grandma Rosie taught us well not to carry sand inside," she called when she passed the piano. Suddenly, she jerked around. "What was that? Something just touched me." She came back out to join her friends.

"What?" Jenny stood and peered behind Faye. "There's nothing there."

"Is it a creepy-crawly spider touching your ear with long legs?" Billie went around Faye and inspected her back.

"A spider?" Faye shivered.

"Only a strand of dried seaweed." Billie picked a wispy green strand from Faye's hair and held it up. "See? It tickled your neck."

"Oh, man." Faye took the strand and released it into the breeze. It fluttered through the air and sailed to the ground. "I'm seeing ghosts."

"Ghosts?" Jenny rubbed her arms. "Are you serious?"

"Faye, it was just a bit of seaweed," Billie said calmly. "Let's not freak each other out."

"That's right; it was just seaweed." Faye went into the living room, and Jenny and Billie followed her.

"It had better be," Jenny murmured. She had to stay in the Forgotten Cove when Faye and Billie left. She couldn't have ghost stories on her mind.

Billie checked her phone. "Kids, I said I would have dinner with Jon. He's cooking, and he takes it seriously. I can't blow him off. It'd be bad for his self-esteem."

Faye laughed as if the danger to Jon's self-esteem was a joke, but Jenny looked up.

"Jon is still around too?" Jenny asked. She remembered Billie's big brother, Jonathan, well enough. He had his own circle of friends and no time to pay his little sister and her friends much attention. But he'd been friendly when their paths did cross, generous to the little girls with his pocket money, and ready to help them out of a tight spot when they needed an independent witness to validate some unlikely excuse.

Of course, they'd all adored him.

One time in particular, Jenny slipped and fell and sprained her ankle when she climbed farther into the cliff than she was allowed. Everyone searched for her when she didn't come home for dinner as promised. It was Jon who heard her calls and who carried her back home all the way over the headlands. Once the good deed was done, Jon returned to politely ignoring the girls. But Jenny's heart had never been quite the same again.

"Jon's very much still around," Billie confirmed now. "Remember my uncle Tommy? Jon bought his vineyard and built a winery."

Billie's uncle Tommy was a freight ship captain and the black sheep of the family. In a singular stroke of luck, he won a vineyard in a late-night poker game at The Salty Dog. As far as Jenny was aware, he never turned a single one of the plump purple grapes into wine.

Only once or twice a year, Captain Tommy would make a sudden appearance in Mendocino Cove. Then he'd load all the kids roaming the village into his beat-up Dodge pickup truck, drive them out to the vineyard, and tell them to eat the grapes they wanted and fill their sand buckets with the rest to bring home.

Jenny smiled at the memory. "How is that going for Jon?" she asked.

"Good. He makes a lot of good wine, and his winery has become a bit of a local hangout spot." Billie said. "It's a lot of hard work and not much money, but it's getting better every year. He just bought the adjacent hills and added them to the vineyard. Jon knows what to do with the plants and the soil. It's a whole science in itself."

"That's great." Jenny liked to picture her childhood hero as a vintner. The occupation fit him.

Faye coughed. "It's dusty in here, isn't it?"

"It is," Jenny confirmed. "It'll take a few days to air out the hotel."

"Did you open the windows upstairs yet?"

"I haven't been upstairs at all. I only just arrived." Jenny looked over her shoulder as if she, too, had seaweed caught in her hair. She laughed, unsure. "I think you got me spooked. I thought someone touched my shoulder too. Brrr." She rubbed the gooseflesh on her arms. "It's been a long day. I'm probably just tired."

Faye tilted her head. "Do you want to stay with me tonight? We'll make a nice dinner. You can go grocery shopping tomorrow morning and then come back to tackle the dust."

"Um." Now that Jenny's friends were about to leave, the hotel suddenly felt big and empty. Spending the night meant being alone with her ghosts—or rather, her thoughts. She'd be listening to every creak and crack, wondering if she was truly alone. She swallowed. "Do you mind, Faye?"

"Of course not. We still have so much catching up to do."

Together, they closed the glass doors and pulled the curtains back in place while Billie washed the glasses and the little snack plate in a kitchen sink full of cold, soapy water.

A few minutes later, Jenny turned the bearded key the other way and locked the hotel again. The afternoon was getting late, and there was a lilt of evening in the rosy sky and the cooling air. "I'm tired," Jenny admitted when she lugged her duffle bag into the trunk of her car. "It was a long journey."

"A long way and a lot of memories. I understand." Faye climbed into Billie's truck and rolled down the window. "Why aren't you driving with us?"

"I'd better take my own car." Jenny pointed at the rental. "That way, I can get back here tomorrow without having to ask for another ride."

Faye smiled softly, as if there was something Jenny fundamentally didn't understand, but didn't insist. "Follow Billie." Faye waved. "She'll drop me off at my house."

"I will?" Billie asked good-naturedly.

"Yep. I haven't had enough lunch to power my legs." Faye rested her elbow on the open window. "See you in ten, Jenny."

Jenny stepped back into the shade of the cypress. "See you, Faye. And guys..." She hesitated.

Billie started the truck and leaned forward so she could see around Faye. "What?" she called over the rumbling engine.

"Thanks for coming over," Jenny called back. "Thanks for stopping by."

"Sure thing!" Billie engaged the clutch. "I'll wait for you at the stop light!"

Kicking up dust like a stubborn mule, the old truck lumbered out of the driveway and onto Forgotten, following the narrow lane to the street to Mendocino Cove.

Jenny turned for a last look at her hotel and did a double take.

Was someone holding open the upstairs curtain?

She stared hard at it, trying to decide whether the curtain hung naturally crooked or whether it was pulled aside. But the breeze swayed the branches of the cypress in a dance as old as the coast, and shadow and light flickered across the windows. It was impossible to tell whether someone was lifting the curtain. Maybe it was just a trick of the eye.

Jenny slammed the trunk shut and hurried to sit in the driver's seat.

Trick or dance, ghost or fluttering strand of seaweed—tomorrow, she would arm herself with a broom and carefully check the bedrooms and attic.

Jenny left, glad for old friends, worried about ghosts, and sorry to leave her house, even if it was only for the night. Above all, she was grateful beyond words that she was back home.

Jenny drove up Forgotten, catching Billie's truck at the stoplight before she turned out toward Mendocino Cove.

CHAPTER 12

E ven on her second drive-through, it was as if the small town had not changed at all since Jenny left. For all she could tell, the yellow and blue lupines and wild roses growing along the same weathered white fences were the same ones she'd picked as a kid for her Mother's Day bouquets. The same lavender seaside daisies bloomed among the waving coastal grasses, and the same orange poppies dotted the headland. Every home, every garden, every shop looked like a long-lost relative.

Jenny followed Billie through a sprinkle of streets until the truck stopped at the curb on Cormorant Lane. Faye jumped out, waved, and slammed the door. Then the truck left again.

Jenny parked in the vacated spot and got out.

Cormorant Lane was a narrow road that ran down a narrow peninsula. With a view of the ocean from almost every window and garden, the lane was one of the prettiest places in Mendocino Cove, with some of the prettiest Victorian houses. For no good reason, Jenny felt surprised—it was such a huge upgrade from Faye's childhood apartment on Main Street.

"The town still looks the same," Jenny said when she pulled her bag from the car. "It's like I never left."

"I don't know about that." Faye smiled. "I *think* I remember old Mr. Whitaker painting his pink gable green ten years ago. The entire town was in shock."

"All in all, that's not too bad." Jenny closed the trunk and hitched her bag higher on her shoulder. "Though naturally, I'm shocked, too. I liked the pink."

"No worries. By now, the green is the same weathered color that the pink used to be," Faye confessed. "Pro tip: if you ever have to name one place where time stands still, say Mendocino Cove. But I like it that way. Most of the time, anyway."

"I like it too. It's very comforting." Jenny followed Faye up the path leading through the front yard. It was dotted with wild lupines and flowering rhododendrons all the way up to the yellow house with white shutters that waited at the end.

"This is your home?" Jenny was already falling in love with the place. She didn't need to see the inside to know it would be just as adorable.

Faye sighed happily. "Billie's uncle sold it to me.

"Captain Tommy? The one who won the vineyard in a game of cards?"

"His twin, Harry Donovan. There were two of them, remember?"

"Oh, yes! The other twin owned a lumberyard, right?"

Slowly, the memories of Billie's populous family returned.

Nothing like his unsteady brother, the captain, Harry had been of the serious and stubborn and strong variety. He ran the lumberyard with his two sons, who were also identical twins. The sons were less serious, but just as stubborn and strong as their father. Jenny couldn't remember their names. Wes? Les? Lester? They had been too old to qualify as playmates, so she hadn't paid the twins much attention. Their talk of machines and lumber and trucks had been too ruggedly masculine and not nearly as interesting as exploring cliff caves or finding gull nests or even, in a pinch, popping bubble algae.

Faye nodded. "Yes, Harry still owns the lumberyard and runs it with his son, Brock. The other brother, Lex, lives near Yosemite Park. He's a ranger there. Do you remember him?"

"Maybe a little. I never had too much to do with the twins. So Harry sold you the house? I imagine not too many houses with views like these come on the market."

"Usually, families hand them on from one generation to the next." Faye pulled out a key. "I got lucky. Sort of." She unlocked the door and went inside.

Before tugging her bag over the threshold, Jenny cast a last look at the ocean. The golden afternoon sky had turned red and pink.

"Tomorrow, we'll have a fire and dinner at the beach," Faye promised and gently closed the door behind them. "Today, you look like you need a quiet evening. Are you tired?"

Jenny set the suitcase down in the entrance and kicked off her shoes. "I am," she admitted. "I'm so tired; I'm not even hungry for dinner."

"We don't have to go out," Faye reassured her. "But we'll have a bite anyway. You don't want to chase exhaustion with late-night hunger."

Jenny nodded. "This is a lovely home," she said.

Her and Stan's house had also been a Victorian. Much larger and statelier than this. But not as charming and nowhere near as cozy.

"Um, Faye, does anyone else live here?" Jenny felt embarrassed to ask. She should know; she should have stayed in touch with friends as good as Faye and Billie. But all the way across the nation, Mendocino Cove had been so far removed from her life with Stan, more dream than reality. "I'm afraid I don't know whether you are married."

"No," Faye said. "No one's caught me yet." She flicked on the light, pulled her purse strap off, and tossed the purse on a table. Then she shook out her curls in front of a delicate white mirror that matched the table.

"I'm sorry I didn't stay in touch," Jenny murmured. "I should have done better."

"We all had plenty to deal with without writing letters." Faye sighed. "Don't worry about that, Jen. We can't all do all the things all the time. Sometimes, we need to drop a ball to juggle the rest. I'm glad you're here now."

It wasn't in Faye's nature to be mad. Jenny could think of only a handful of instances over the years of their friendship where she had seen her truly angry. "Thanks, Faye," she said.

"And don't worry about Billie growling. She likes to keep everyone where she can see them, but she'll calm down. Her entire family is pathologically loyal and local. It's a genetic glitch. She's working on it."

Jenny nodded. "Okay."

"Jonathan will want to see you," Faye added casually. "We might stop by and say hi before you leave again. What do you think?"

"Sure."

"Maybe we can go tomorrow, pick up some wine for the bonfire dinner while we're there."

Jenny rubbed her hands. The tips of her fingers suddenly tingled from carrying the heavy duffle bag. "Sounds good."

"Well." Faye smiled. "Come on in." She waved Jenny into a charming room with wide floorboards of soft honey pine and white walls. There were hutches and shelves and woven baskets full of things. A long farm table stood in the center. It, too, was covered with things. Graceful bronze figurines and silver trays and stacks of old books and blue-and-white tea pots and milky-green glass vases. In the corners of the room stood comfy armchairs upholstered in cheerful fabrics beside luscious, large potted ferns. Variegated spider plants dropped their spring green spiderlings down the sides of the antique pine hutches.

"What a lovely room!" Jenny couldn't help but pick up a small pair of silver scissors from the table and admire them. "How intricate!"

"This is my little store of all things lost and found and loved." Jenny looked up and saw Faye watching her intently. "Do you like the scissors?"

"I do," Jenny said. "I've never seen anything so..." She tried to find the right words. Of course, she'd seen Victorian sewing scissors before. They, too, had leaves and vines engraved along the handle, and they, too, had been dainty and silver. But these scissors drew her to them. She turned them over, unsure how to finish the sentence. There was nothing special about the scissors.

"Take them," Faye said. "They look good on you."

"I can't just take them. You're running a business." Jenny wanted to set the scissors back down. Instead, she turned them over again as if she'd missed something the first time.

"It's all right."

"At least let me pay for them." Jenny had very little cash for antique sewing scissors.

"Just take them already." Faye shook her head at the offer of payment. "I don't take money when it's love at first sight."

CHAPTER 13

I imagine it's hard to make a living with a secondhand store." Feeling shy, Jenny pocketed the scissors. She needed them. Why, she had no idea.

Faye lifted the lid of a glazed teapot and peered inside, then set it back. "It's enough," she said distractedly. "Sort of."

Jenny tilted her head to read the names of the stacked books. They were vintage editions of a famous old children's series about adventures. Jenny had loved the series when she was little, and her heart still lifted when she saw the familiar titles. Beside the books stood an antique blue-and-white china platter. Jenny had seen it many times on the dinner table.

"You have treasure everywhere," she said and ran a finger along the side of the tray. "This is beautiful. Grandma used to own one just like it."

Faye glanced at her. "Do you want it?"

Touched, Jenny shook her head. "If there's anything the hotel has enough of, it's china and linen. But thank you for offering." Her hand went to her pocket with the scissors. They were still there.

Faye nodded.

"What's over here?" Jenny couldn't stop looking. There was so much to see, and the longer she looked, the more there seemed to be, as if things multiplied every time she looked away. Jenny loved thrift stores and could spend hours searching through them.

Far from being stuffy like some thrift stores where things were tossed helter-skelter onto shelves and bins, Faye had given every item love and attention, finding it a place where it could shine.

Jenny now remembered that it was always Faye who found things. Faye found baby birds and squirrels who needed a hand to get back in the nest. Faye found lost balls and toys and even a lost dollar bill that Billie was supposed to hand in for a school trip. It had fluttered out of the pocket of her shorts and gotten lodged under a tree. As if they revealed themselves only to her, Faye always spotted the best sea glass, the bush with the largest huckleberries, the flattest sitting rocks.

Faye wiggled the lid back on the teapot. "Let me close the windows. The evening air is getting cool. We can make a fire in the fireplace upstairs, and I can tell you about the shop—and the other thing I do."

"That sounds nice." Even if the days were hot, mid-May was still a good time for evening fires.

Faye led the way through another room. It was simply furnished but cozy with plump white cushions in the window seats and built-in bookshelves that framed an antique fireplace. A small crystal vase with two orange California poppies stood on a small white table be-tween two cozy armchairs. Almost everything in the room was white, but the light of the sinking sun cast everything in hues of red and pink and purple.

"What a view you have." Jenny went to the window to admire the sea that spread like molten bronze below the bluff.

"It's no different from the view from your hotel." Faye smiled. "I've never forgotten the evenings there. Sundowns at the hotel feel like standing in the middle of the sea when the sea goes down. Color everywhere."

"I never forgot them either."

"Come up the stairs. Down here is my shop and my meeting room. Upstairs is where I live."

A meeting room? There was so much Jenny still didn't know. "You have a kitchen upstairs?" Jenny fetched her bag and followed Faye up the elegant curve of the stairs.

"I do. There was a second kitchen downstairs, but I took out the wall to make the store. The house used to belong to the Norman sisters. Lizabeth had good legs and lived upstairs, kitchen and all. Nelly had the downstairs."

"I think I remember them."

"They passed away only a month apart. There were no heirs, but Nelly had been good friends with Billie's uncle Harry, and her will gave him first dibs at buying the house. He meant to convert it to a single house for...well." Faye sighed. "For me, I suppose. And Lex."

"Lex?"

"The one who lives near Yosemite? We were engaged to be married before he moved." Faye opened a door on the landing. "Harry sold us the house. Lex and I lived here for a year before he left."

"What happened?" Jenny set her bag down by the stairs and stepped into a room that was as bright and cheerful as the ones downstairs.

The walls with their white wainscoting were painted a soft green that beautifully reflected the last of the fading evening light. A pair of yellow upholstered armchairs stood in front of a fireplace, and a variety of paintings of flowers and birds hung on the walls. Here, too, tall plants softened the corners, and braided baskets full of books stood by the chairs.

"For now, let's just say Lex and I didn't work out. So. Are you going to be okay sleeping on the sofa? I only have one bedroom up here since the rest are downstairs. It's a small house, after all."

"Of course." The sofa was really a fainting divan. It stood pushed against the wall under a tall window. When Jenny went to sit on it, she saw the blue and green pheasants and peacocks stitched into the soft red of the fabric. "Faye, this is beautiful." She ran her fingers over the birds. "Are you sure I should be sleeping on it? It looks precious."

"Of course you should sleep on it. I'll put sheets on it and make it cozy for you. It's not half as fragile as it looks, and you'll have a wonderful view of the moon. Come, I'll show you the rest of the rooms. There aren't many more."

"Yes, please." Jenny looked at Faye's own pretty bedroom, the sparkling clean bathroom with a small pedestal sink and a large claw-footed tub, the kitchen with the breakfast corner overlooking the ocean where the tour ended. "I can't imagine a place feeling more like your home than this," Jenny said.

"I poured my heart into fixing it. I can't imagine living anywhere else ever again." Faye lit the flame on the gas stove and nodded for Jenny to sit in the breakfast nook. "I have clam chowder with rosemary potatoes and sourdough bread. Sounds good?"

"Sounds very good." Jenny sank onto the bench and folded her hands. "How can I help?"

Faye turned her head to grin over her shoulder. "By doing what you're doing right now. This isn't the hotel kitchen—there's just enough space for one. You sit, and we'll have a nice glass of wine while I heat the soup."

Jenny relaxed. The night in the hotel would have been beautiful too. But the grand old house would have been cold and dusty and spooky. Here, everything was bright and charming and warm.

"Look, this is wine from Jon's vineyard. His reds and whites are both good, but I feel like white wine tonight." Faye filled a tall glass and set it in front of Jenny. "Do you want sesame crackers and cheese with it? I have a nice mellow goat cheese log."

"My husband killed himself a year ago." Jenny looked up, shocked. She hadn't meant to say the words. They had come out of nowhere.

CHAPTER 14

"Oh no, Jen." Faye's eyes widened. "I'm so sorry."

Jenny touched her lips as if she could take the words back. "I don't know why I said that. I didn't mean to bring it up." She had learned long ago that she couldn't dump her worries whenever she felt like it. Only good things that could be posted on Facebook were for sharing. The rest was to be carried in silence.

Maybe if you had family, you could tell them. But Jenny had no family left.

None that listened, anyway.

For a moment, Faye was silent.

Jenny inhaled to apologize again and do her best to play the awkward comment off when Faye finally said, "We'll talk, Jen. Let's first have a glass of cold wine and a bowl of warm soup. Then we'll make a fire, and you can tell me what happened, all right?"

Jenny lowered her hand again. "All right," she murmured, not sure she would take Faye up on the offer. But maybe she should. Maybe Faye would find the words Jenny couldn't find on her own.

"Okay." Faye lifted her own glass, and they both drank. "Are you okay?" Faye asked then.

Jenny shrugged. "Sometimes I don't know *what* I am. I barely know who I am."

"You're Jenny," Faye said and pulled a large pot from the fridge. "And you've come back home."

Jenny's phone dinged, and she pulled it out. It was a text from Audrey. "It's my daughter," she said.

"You have a daughter?" Faye pulled a large pot from the fridge and set it on the stove. Then she lit the flame, pulled a long wooden spoon from a drawer, and started stirring the fragrant clam chowder.

"Her name is Audrey. She studies hotel management," Jenny said. "I also have a son. His name is River. He's doing his residency for medical school."

"Audrey and River." Faye smiled. "You must be proud of them."

"So very." Jenny smiled back. "Do you mind if I text Audrey? I didn't tell them about this trip before I left. River takes things in stride, but she sounds worried." Her heart sank in her chest. "The thing is, my husband cheated his clients out of a lot of money. I only learned about it a few months ago, when there was an investigation and it all came out. I lost everything, including my house. The kids don't know about any of it yet—I want Audrey to finish the semester first. She's graduating, and there's no reason to throw her off so close to her final exams."

"Whoa," Faye whispered. "I'm sorry, Jenny."

"I just need a bit of time to get back on my feet." Jenny didn't want to be dramatic. She still had her kids and an aunt and a hotel in Mendocino Cove.

"Go ahead and text your Audrey. Of course I don't mind." Faye pulled out a basket of potatoes from a cupboard and started picking through them, throwing the ones she wanted into a colander for washing.

Jenny took a deep drink of the crisp wine and read the new text.

Mostly, her daughter wanted to know whether Jenny had arrived at the hotel. She asked for photos too. Audrey was clearly suspicious of her mother's trip to Mendocino Cove.

Jenny snapped a quick selfie with the sun sinking into the ocean as the background, then wrote a few cheery lines about having dinner with a friend and staying over until the hotel was clean and aired out. Then she forwarded both text and photo to River.

Audrey immediately shot back a reply. She sounded relieved Jenny wasn't alone and had already connected with old friends. She asked for a call soon and reported that her exams were looming.

Jenny texted back and forth until Audrey sounded reassured, and then she put down the phone and emptied her glass.

Wordlessly, Faye refilled it. "The potatoes are done," she reported and pulled the roasting sheet from the oven, setting it on the stove top and poking a golden-brown wedge with a fork. "And so are the bread and the clam chowder. Are you ready to eat?"

Jenny wasn't hungry, but the lovely cooking smells of clam chowder and sourdough bread, roasted rosemary potatoes, and warm olive oil could have seduced a toddler into trying the foods. "Yes, I am." She tucked the phone away. "I'm suddenly hungry too."

"I hope so. A couple of crackers only tie over a grown woman for so long." Faye set two bowls of steaming chowder and two plates with perfectly roasted potatoes and bread on the table. Then she dropped into the chair and grinned at Jenny. "Tadaa."

"Thank you so much," Jenny said. "It smells incredible."

Faye lifted her glass. "Cheers, my dear. I'm so glad you're back."

Jenny lifted her glass too. "Cheers, Faye. I'm so glad you found me."

She winked. "It's what I do."

They took their time to savor their dinner.

"I put garlic on the potatoes," Faye said contentedly and emptied her glass. "Good thing we don't have to kiss anyone tonight,"

"That's one way to see it." Jenny smiled.

"Come on, let's have that fire." Faye stood and started collecting the dishes.

"I'll do the washing up," Jenny said and joined her. "I cannot just sit there and drink wine and watch you labor."

"Oh, with the drama. Fine. There's dish soap and a sponge under the sink. Knock yourself out. I'll make us a fire in the meantime."

Jenny hummed as she washed the dishes. After she polished the last spoon and put it back into its drawer, she hung up the towel to dry and went to look for

Faye. She found her friend sitting in one of the yellow armchairs in front of a crackling fire, an enormous cat stretched across her lap, her feet on an ottoman.

Jenny sat in the other chair. On the little table between them stood two new glasses and a bottle of red wine, as well as a plate with soft rounds of goat cheese, fresh figs, and candied walnuts.

"Pour," Faye said softly, petting the cat.

Jenny poured. She'd already had two glasses of white wine, but the rich food seemed to have soaked up the alcohol. She was tired but felt more clear-headed than she had in months. "Who's your friend?"

"I don't know."

CHAPTER 15

F aye tore her gaze from the dancing fire to look at the massive cat that not only filled her lap but spilled over like a fur blanket. "It's strange that he looks so striking and yet nobody knows whom he belongs to. But he's in fine shape, so I'm not worried for him."

The tufts on the cat's ears reminded Jenny of a lynx. "Does he have a name?"

The cat turned his gaze on Jenny, and she was startled to find that his eyes were as yellow as the armchairs.

"Personally, I call him Tantor. He sometimes visits me in the evenings." Faye let her hand glide over the fur from the ears to the tail. "He jumps in through the window and comes to sit here. Not all the time, but more often than not." She tickled the fuzzy chin, but the large cat ignored her. "I miss him when he doesn't visit."

"Do you feed him?"

"I offer him treats, but he doesn't always take them. Not even fresh tuna."

Jenny smiled. "Just a beautiful friendship then." Faye petted the thick, long fur, and static sparks flew in the air. Jenny blinked. She was tired. Maybe the sparks, like the moving curtain earlier, had been a trick of the flickering light.

"Yes," Faye said. "It's a heartwarming friendship, as long as I don't do anything he doesn't approve of. He can be judgmental. But he seems to like you." She picked up her glass and took a sip, and then she asked Jenny about Stan and the house and the kids, and Jenny leaned back into her chair and answered. Answers turned into stories, and suddenly a dam broke, and the words flowed like a creek that had been looking for a path for a long time.

The cat watched with moon eyes until Jenny was done talking. She felt empty and hollow now that the words had drained and sank back into her chair.

Tantor rested his head on his paws.

"How do you feel right now?" Faye asked after a while.

"My legs fell asleep, but my toes are nice and warm." Jenny wiggled them as the blood flooded back into them.

"You still have your kids," Faye said gently. "You have yourself."

"That is true," Jenny said. "I have the kids, but I'm so terribly scared something will happen to them too."

Faye sighed. "Trust catches late but burns bright. When you think none of it can possibly have survived, it pokes out its seedling head and grows again."

"Let's hope the bit about the seedling is true. I don't want to live in fear anymore."

Faye shifted, and the big cat on her lap purred. "It sounds corny, but coming here might help you. When Lex broke off our engagement, the cove saved my sanity."

"Sitting on the rocks with you and Billie earlier gave me a little bit of hope," Jenny admitted.

"Hope for what?" Faye turned to look at her.

The fire had burned down, and Jenny could barely see her friend in the dark. "I don't know," she said. "Just hope."

Tantor suddenly stood and arched his back, stretching before he jumped to the ground. Quiet as a shadow, he left the room.

"He's going home, wherever that is." Faye stood and brushed cat hair off her lap. "We should go to bed too. You must be dead on your feet."

Tiredness settled on Jenny like a mantle, pressing on her eyes and opening her mouth in a great big yawn. "I am. Not even the jet lag helps."

"Let me put sheets on the couch. You go ahead and use the bathroom."

"Thanks, Faye." Gratefully, Jenny brushed her teeth and put on her night shirt while Faye put fresh sheets on the divan and fluffed a cozy duvet and pillows.

"I put more wood on the fire so you're warm and have some light to fall asleep to." Faye pointed at the small fire in the fireplace. "I closed the flue a bit, so it'll last you. Good night."

"Good night." Jenny curled up in her comfy bed. The moon was shining silvery into the window overhead, and a myriad of stars twinkled in the velvety blue sky. "Hey, Faye?"

Faye turned in the door, wine glasses in hand. "Yeah?"

"You said you would tell me what you do. It sounded like it wasn't just about the store." Jenny propped herself on her elbow. "What exactly is it you do besides selling secondhand things?"

"Oh. There isn't a good name for it." Faye scratched her chin. "People come to talk to me."

"What do you mean?"

"I noticed that people came to browse the store but stayed to talk. Sometimes about private things, things you wouldn't necessarily share with a store owner. I thought it was just a glitch, but it kept happening. People came back too, ready to talk more."

"You are easy to talk to." Jenny smiled. "You always were a good listener."

"At first I was scared. Did I want to know all these things?"

"Well, did you?" Jenny asked.

"I got used to it. I put armchairs in the other room so we could sit and wouldn't have to whisper quite so low for other customers not to hear."

"I never heard of something like that."

"You're telling me." Faye sighed. "Next thing, people insisted on bringing little gifts or leaving donations. A plate of cupcakes here, a five-dollar bill tucked under their teacup there."

"That's even stranger," Jenny said.

"I told them not to give me things in the beginning, but people didn't listen. Little Mrs. Simon
is the sweetest person in the world, always telling
me stories about her grandchild and his pet bunny.
But when I said I didn't want her lemon cakes, she
whacked my shin with her walking stick."

"Oh no." Jenny bit back a laugh. "And you used to
like lemon cake, didn't you?"

"I still do. Eventually, Billie said to just let people pay for my time. It makes them feel like they
can come back to talk more without imposing." She
shrugged. "Some weeks I make more from listening
than from selling things."

"Almost like a therapist."

"Only I'm not. I rarely know what to tell them,
and often enough I don't even understand them. I'm
just sitting there. I'm just someone to talk to." She
shrugged. "Why people want to do it in the first
place—I have no idea. Maybe it's the house."

The house did have a cheerful, open atmosphere
that made you want to stay and relax and let down
your guard. "*I* just told you everything that I've never
said out loud to anyone," Jenny said.

"And?" Faye smiled. "How does that make you
feel?" She adjusted imaginary glasses on her nose.

Jenny smiled back. "Good."

"There you go then." Faye started to close the
door. "We'll talk more tomorrow. Sleep in, okay? I
know I will." The door closed softly.

"Good night, cove," Jenny whispered as she settled back into her soft bed. Above, the stars twinkled as if they knew a secret and were bursting to tell.

Tomorrow, Jenny would go back to the hotel and check out the upstairs. Make sure it wasn't wild raccoons who were haunting the place.

The fire danced a sleepy dance, and the moon watched from above as Jenny's eyelids fluttered close and she felt herself drifting into a sea of seedling hopes and evergreen dreams.

CHAPTER 16

"A nyone home?" Billie knocked on the door again. Faye and Jenny hadn't gone out for breakfast, had they? She checked her watch. It was barely nine—and unlike Billie, Faye was definitely not a morning person.

A moment later, the door opened. "Hey." Faye blinked into the sunlight, which was hazy with the last of the morning fog. She was wearing an old T-shirt and baggy gray sweatpants. "What's up, Bills?"

"Hey." Billie squeezed past Faye into the house. She hadn't brought a sweater, and her bare arms were covered in goose skin. She rubbed them. "Brrr. It's only just warming up out there. Good morning."

"Oof." Faye closed the door behind Billie. "You're right."

Every morning, Billie woke up at five at the latest. She had coffee and listened to an audiobook while she prepared the most important meal of the day. It was her morning meditation. Once whatever was on the menu was baked, fried, or grilled, Billie fed the animals in her charge before she had her own breakfast. More often than not, her friends came to have breakfast with her.

"Hey, hey, hey, lookie what I have here." She held up the bag of bagels she'd brought and inhaled involuntarily. The freshly baked bread smelled delicious, and she hadn't had breakfast yet. "Brekkie time."

"What?" Faye took the bag without seeming to understand what it was.

"Goodness, Faye, wake up already. It's nine o'clock, practically the middle of the day. I bought bagels for breakfast." Billie grabbed Faye's shoulders dramatically. "Do you understand?"

Faye's eyebrows dropped. "How many cups of coffee have you had already?"

"Seven." Billie took the bagels back and went upstairs. Faye was hopeless in the morning. "Is Jenny still here?" she called over her shoulder.

Faye mumbled something and toddled after her. Billie cracked open the door to the living room. There was Jenny, sleeping on the sofa. Softly, Billie closed the door again and went into the kitchen to check the fridge for eggs. There were plenty of eggs and thick rashers of maple bacon. By the time Billie had scrambled eggs and fried the bacon and brewed coffee, Faye reappeared.

Her hair was wet from the shower, and she was dressed in jeans and a heather-colored fleece sweater.

"Good morning, Billie." Faye slid into the breakfast nook and stuffed a pillow behind her back. "I see you found my grass-fed bacon."

"Good morning, again. Finally awake, huh?" Billie set down a plate full of eggs and bacon and a bagel with cream cheese and honey. "How are you doing?"

"I'm fine." Faye cleared her throat. "I hope I wasn't rude. I'm not responsible for my actions before eleven."

"You wish." Billie set another loaded plate on the table. "Jenny is still asleep?"

"She's in the shower."

"Here." Billie poured coffee and pushed a large mug in front of Faye. "I don't know what would happen to you if I wouldn't take care of you in the mornings," she said critically.

"You don't take care of me in the mornings. Last time we had breakfast together was at least two weeks ago." Faye picked up her steaming mug. "I know why you're here."

Billie poured another mug for herself, filled a third place, and sat on the bench next to Faye. "Oh yeah?"

"Yeah. I already asked on your behalf." Faye slurped her brew.

Billie sank back and closed her eyes. "You're a true friend. Yes?"

"Yes."

"You want my bacon?"

"You mean, do I want more of my bacon? No thanks. I'm trying to survive middle age."

The floor creaked, and Jenny appeared in the open door. Her hair was tied up in a ponytail. She was dressed in a white blouse and skinny jeans but wore no makeup or socks. "Hey. Good morning, Billie."

"Morning. Do you want some breakfast?" Billie pointed at the plate and got up to pour another mug of coffee.

"Thank you." Jenny took the coffee with both hands and drank, then sat on the chair and pulled the plate over. "Looks delicious, but I really hope you didn't go to the trouble because of me."

"It's no trouble, Jen." Billie sat back down and bit off the end of a rasher of bacon. "Did you sleep well?"

Jenny nodded. "I did." She tried her scrambled eggs. "Uh. Yummy."

"What do you two want to do today?" Billie asked when Faye had finished her food and leaned back.

Jenny put the last of her bagel with cream cheese and honey in her mouth. "I need to do some grocery shopping and spend a few hours cleaning the hotel."

Billie nodded. "What about your rental car? Are you going to keep it?"

Jenny pressed her lips into a line. "I can't. It's too expensive."

"Yeah?" Involuntarily, Billie glanced at the designer blouse.

"I was telling Faye about my situation last night. I lost pretty much everything but my kids and whatever is in my duffle bag." Jenny looked up. "I had a few rough months."

"Tell me." Billie got up and refilled the mugs before sitting down again. "Catch me up."

Jenny did. Now and then, Faye added something she'd learned the night before.

"Oh, Jenny," Billie said when Jenny was done. She had figured that something in Jenny's life had gone awry for her finally to return home. But Billie hadn't imagined a tragedy. "I wish I could help."

Jenny smiled her appreciation for the sentiment. "The damage is done. I'm all right." She folded her hands. "I just need to catch my breath."

"I understand."

"I suppose I also need to figure out what to do about money," Jenny said. "My safety net has ripped. The retirement fund is gone. So are the savings."

Billie had heard this story before. The reasons differed, but a handful of middle-aged women in her acquaintance, whose life had been built around their kids and marriages, suddenly found themselves alone and penniless.

The good news was that every one of them had survived their crash landing. The better news was that they all were happier for starting over. Maybe they had less money and smaller houses. But cut free by those they used to put first, they enjoyed discovering who they had become since last checking in with themselves.

"What about your mom's inheritance? Did it all go to your aunt?" Billie asked.

"I received my mother's share. It went to pay for my and the kids' tuition. None of us picked colleges for their cheap tuition."

"Nothing left over?"

"Back in the eighties, the hotel wasn't worth a fraction of what it is worth now." Jenny smiled.

"Georgie lucked out by not selling back then, huh?" Faye picked up a sesame seed with the tip of her finger and thoughtfully ate it.

Jenny nodded. "I'm glad she didn't sell it. I can't stand the thought of losing it."

"I thought your aunt was supposed to take care of you." Billie frowned. "The hotel property alone would be worth a small fortune, let alone the house."

"My aunt doesn't take care of people. People take care of her," Jenny said lightly. "At least she lets me stay at the hotel. She didn't like the thought, though. I think she would prefer if the hotel was as forgotten as the cove."

Billie shook her head but bit her tongue. Neither Georgie nor Jenny had been in a good way when they left Mendocino Cove for Nantucket. Billie had always worried about Jenny being in her aunt's care. Billie had always had a solid network of family and friends, and it worried her when one of them fell out of touch. She couldn't imagine being forced to leave the cove.

"Why didn't you come to your grandmother's funeral? I was hoping to see you there." She'd wanted to ask this question for many years.

CHAPTER 17

Audrey was due two weeks after Rosie died. I was much too pregnant to be allowed on an airplane. I had hoped Georgie would go since she'd organized the funeral. But she couldn't face it."

"Oh. I'm sorry." A pregnancy hadn't occurred to Billie. "You have kids, huh?"

Jenny nodded, her gaze far away. "Two." She quickly caught Billie up.

Faye reached over, pulled a rasher of bacon from Jenny's plate, and started nibbling on it.

Jenny pushed her plate toward her. She'd not eaten much. "I have to get a job; it doesn't matter what as long as it pays. Did you hear about anyone looking for help?"

"I wish I did." Billie shook her head, sorry she couldn't help. But Mendocino Cove was a small town. Like the houses with the best ocean views, jobs making a living wage stayed in the families who created them. "Did you finish a degree?"

Jenny's eyes brightened. "I have a PhD from Pequod University in Nantucket. It never did me much good, but I do have it."

"Whoa." Faye stuffed the last bit of bacon in her mouth and wiped her hands on a napkin. "In what?"

"History."

"Yes!" Billie stopped short of pumping a hand into the air. "I knew it, Faye!"

"No, *I* knew it." Faye grinned. "You were always interested in mummies and stuff, boring us to tears when you went off. Well done, Jen."

Billie sat up straight. "You could be a professor at Elizabeth May University. It's only twenty minutes from here, and you'd be good at teaching. Plus, you could research all the old things in Faye's store."

"They're not *that* old," Faye said mildly. "I stay clear of pilfered mummies."

"Good on you." Jenny chuckled, but then she sobered. "It's been a long time since I last published anything—or knew anyone. I'm out of the loop. Unfortunately, academia is a highly competitive job market."

"What job market isn't?" Faye was scrolling on her phone. "They do have a history department. But I don't see any job postings."

"I wouldn't have a chance, anyway."

"What was it about?" Billie asked after a moment. "Your last publication?"

"Shipwrecks and things like that." Jenny smiled fondly and emptied her coffee cup. "Nantucket's coast is littered with sunken ships. Whaling was huge back in the day, and the shore is dangerous."

"I like a good historical shipwreck." Billie propped her elbows on the table and rested her face in her hands. "Elaborate on 'things like that,' please."

Jenny refilled her cup. "It wasn't so much the wrecks themselves, I'm afraid, but their effects on Nantucket families. What happened when they lost their precious ships—and loved ones?"

"Sweet. I love shipwrecks. And *pirates*." Faye sighed happily. "Not the modern ones, though. The old ones with eye patches and sabers in their belts."

"Cape Cod had the best old pirate of them," Jenny said. "Black Sam Bellamy called himself the Robin Hood of the sea."

"Black Sam Bellamy?" Billie also liked herself a noble olden-times pirate. "Was he handsome?"

"Hmm. If it counts, he preferred his own back hair over a powdered wig."

"So sexy," Faye said dreamily.

Jenny laughed. "I suppose he was all right. According to legend, he started pirating to become rich enough to marry his one true love."

"Aww," Billie and Faye said in unison.

"Well, if you're interested in a love story, you might be interested in my research after all," Jenny said. "It was based on a very scandalous story—a young sailor who eloped with his sweetheart."

"On a boat?" Faye wanted to know.

"On his dad's whaler, a bark called The Provident," Jenny confirmed. "The sailor's name was William Langley, and his sweetheart was Phoebe Seabrook. Unfortunately for the two lovebirds, their families feuded bitterly over the boundaries of their lobster territories. Fortunately for me, after the two got in trouble for speaking to each other, they started writing secret letters to plan their elopement."

"How do you know?" Faye asked.

"I found the letters." Jenny smiled broadly, showing how much she'd loved her research.

"Tell us all the dirty details," Billie encouraged her. Secret love letters were good, and it was even better to see Jenny smile like that.

"It was a windfall, really. My friend Sam owns a bookstore in Maine. She bought a few books that belonged to Phoebe's favorite cousin. Among them was a cookbook and tucked in between the pages were Will's letters to Phoebe. There were also a couple of Phoebe's letters to her cousin about Will. Sam contacted my professor about her find, and my professor asked me to meet Sam and have a look at the letters."

"I bet you went."

Jenny grinned. "What more could I ask for but a pair of lost lovers from two Nantucket whaling families? I *ran* to meet Sam, and let me tell you, it didn't hurt that she lives in Beach Cove. Except for Mendocino Cove, I've never seen a more adorable little seaside town. Her friends put me up in their inn. It reminded me so much of my hotel. I was homesick the entire time. But we've all been friends ever since."

"So Will and his Phoebe eloped?" Faye put her chin in her hand, smiling. "What a total scandal. Tell me more."

Jenny nodded. "One dark, starry night, little six-teen-year-old Phoebe dressed up as a man, and Will snuck her on board. He was only eighteen, but he already had command of The Provident."

"Was it really starry?" Billie wasn't one for embell-ishments, but she quite liked the thought of stars lightening little Phoebe's path. The girl must have been terribly scared, and excited, and very, very much in love with her young whaler.

"So says Phoebe." Jenny smiled. "She wrote to her cousin that Will had arranged for most of the crew to be his friends."

"What about the others?"

"By the time they found out about the unlucky woman on board, it would be too late to return."

"Then what?" Billie asked. "Did Will and Phoebe return to Nantucket, happily married?"

"Uh. No, poor babies. They didn't. Here's where the shipwreck situation comes in." Jenny peered into her empty mug as if answers were to be found in the coffee grounds. "A nasty nor'eastern pushed The Provident on an underwater shoal when she returned, and it ripped open her hull. Like so many other ships around Cape Cod, she sank."

"What? What kind of ending is that?" Billie sat back and crossed her arms. She wasn't romantic. Nobody was less romantic than a woman whose husband had been a cheater. But that ending? No.

Jenny looked contrite. "I don't know what happened to the lovers."

"Oh no." Faye, too, looked crestfallen. "They didn't drown, did they?"

Jenny sighed. "All I could find out is that The Provident was seen in Hawaii before returning to Nantucket."

"*Hawaii*? What?" Faye shook her head as if her ears were failing her.

"A lot of Nantucket whalers traveled to the Pacific to hunt sperm whales. It wasn't so unusual to land somewhere and stretch your legs. I know I would."

"Maybe Will and Phoebe got off in Maui for a proper honeymoon and lived out long and happy lives," Billie said hopefully.

"I know," Jenny said, but she shook her head as if she didn't believe it. "I wish there'd been more letters."

"Our coast has some famous shipwrecks too," Billie said. "As you probably know."

"Of course," Jenny said. "A rugged coast is a rugged coast."

"All that fog doesn't help," Faye said.

"Neither does my PhD." Jenny cleared her throat. "Are you sure the Mermaid Galley doesn't need a waitress?"

"Hannah is more staff than Michael can handle." Faye giggled. "The other places are too small to hire."

"What about the hotel?" Billie propped her arms on the table. "Could you open it back up for business?"

Jenny looked doubtful. "I don't know. Maybe if I go in with a whole presentation to convince my aunt she could make heaps of money. What's the tourism situation like?"

Faye weaved her head. "Not too good. The drought doesn't help. I don't know how your grandmother did it."

"I never thought to ask her. But I doubt she made much profit."

Billie checked her phone. "Jon is going to work out in the vineyard today." She stood. "If we want to buy a bottle or two for the bonfire tonight, we should stop by soon."

"If it's not convenient, I'm all right just going to the supermarket," Jenny said.

Billie looked at Faye, and Faye looked back, a slight smile playing on her lips.

"Forget it," Billie said firmly. Clearly, Jenny had to catch up on how things worked around town. "We're going to the winery."

"Oh. Okay." Jenny looked at her hands, studying her fingernails.

"Let's go. I can drive."

"Yeah, let's go." Faye stood as well. "I'll do the dishes when I get back."

They put on jackets and shoes, and Billie led the way out to the house, making sure Jenny was behind her.

Whatever it took, Billie was going to make Jenny see her brother.

Anything to make Jon finally move on.

CHAPTER 18

Jenny glanced over her shoulder. It wasn't easy, squished as she was between Faye and Billie. They were driving away from the ocean at a speed that couldn't possibly comply with the local limit. Or the old truck's suspension system.

"All right, Billie?" she asked casually.

"Absolutely." Billie flicked the blinker and turned, making everyone sway like poppies in the wind.

Jenny grabbed the dash to steady herself. "Since I talked all morning...what about you?"

"Me? Uh. Let's see. I was married."

"Yeah?" It was only natural that Billie should have married. She was smart and warm and loyal to a fault. If that wasn't enough, she had a smile that could knock any man off his feet and a figure that couldn't be ignored despite the faded T-shirts and jeans.

"Yeah." Billie cleared her throat.

"What happened?" Jenny wanted to know.

"He cheated," Billie said lightly. "While I was at home feeding the boys mashed carrots and peas, he was busy making more. Kids. Not carrots and peas."

"You have *boys*?"

Faye chuckled beside Jenny.

"Two," Billie confirmed. "Louis and Ben. They've both flown the nest; bless their little hearts."

"In case that gives you the impression they're small—they're huge," Faye said. "Ben is enormous."

"I didn't feed them mash for nothing." Billie sounded satisfied.

It took Jenny a moment to arrange the bits and pieces of information. "I feel so stupid for having to ask." She might as well get it over with. "But what is it you do, Billie?"

"I run a small animal rescue station," Billie said cheerfully and pulled the truck to a stop. "If I could, I'd hire you to bottle-feed orphaned sea lion pups. But there's no money."

"I'll help for free."

Billie opened her door and grinned over her shoulder. "It's not all it's cracked up to be." She jumped out.

"No snuggling fuzzy pups?" Jenny wiggled out as well, glad to have survived the break-speed drive.

"They're stinky little things. Fish breath. Besides, they aren't supposed to get used to humans." Billie slammed her door shut. "Luckily, it's not busy right now. I only have a pelican with a nicked wing that's healing nicely. The splint is off, and we're working on physical exercise for his rehabilitation. Did you know that pelican beaks are very sharp?"

"I never thought about it." Jenny joined Faye in the shade of a beautiful old tree and turned to study the gorgeous view. Nestled into the picturesque rolling hills were rows upon rows of neatly tied grapevines, with meandering paths leading to ancient oaks and hidden corners. Beside the winery itself, an expansive shaded terrace overlooked the landscape, and a gentle breeze carried the aroma of blooming lavender and the sweet scent of ripe grapes to Jenny. A meadowlark sang in the azure sky, and oak leaves rustled in the breeze. Jenny couldn't imagine a more tranquil and serene atmosphere.

"This is your brother's vineyard?" she asked, incredulous anyone could own such a slice of paradise. "It's beautiful!"

"Isn't it? He's in there." Billie nodded at the large house ahead of them.

"Oh, boy." Faye smiled expectantly, as if she was looking forward to something.

"What?" Jenny looked around to see what Faye was talking about. There were only the grapevines growing in orderly rows along wooden trellises. "It looks like Italy," she said, enamored. "Stan took me there for our honeymoon."

Billie closed the door of the truck. "Oh, *boy*."

"Why do you two keep saying that?"

Faye shook her head. "Just because the mockingbirds are eating the grapes."

"I don't see any mockingbirds in the grapes." Jenny shaded her eyes and squinted at the vines.

"Let's go in and see Jon before he leaves." Billie checked her phone and started walking toward the house.

Jenny and Faye followed.

"You remember Jon, don't you?" Faye asked.

"I do."

"Remember how he carried you home across the bluff?" The smile in Faye's eyes deepened. "You'd sprained your ankle. He knew your favorite spots and found you."

Jenny smiled. Some of the spots had been her favorites *because* Jon had shown them to her. "I can't believe *you* remember."

"Please. It was the most romantic thing that happened in Mendocino Cove all year."

"Mh-hmm." Decades ago as it was, every moment in Jon's arms had burned itself in Jenny's impressionable young mind. The pain in her ankle had been real, but the sensation paled in comparison to the soft beating of Jon's heart against hers and the easy rhythm of his walk. Even his scent of cedar sap and sun-dried driftwood still lived in her memory.

"I hope he's in so I can say hi," she said. "But I doubt he'll even recognize me."

Just as vividly as the most romantic event of the year, Jenny remembered the least romantic let down. She hadn't expected Jon to like her better for having had to carry her back home. But a visit to ask how she was would have been nice. Concern over the state of her ankle, maybe. "He barely talked to me afterward."

"Oh well. Guys, you know?" Faye swallowed wrong and coughed.

They had caught up with Billie, who held the door open for them.

The vineyard's tasting room was a charming, rustic building made of warm wood, windows, and breathtaking views. Natural light flooded the space, but it was pleasantly cool after the heat in the parking lot.

"It's so pretty," Jenny whispered to Faye. Vintage wine barrels served as tables, and local artwork and cozy seating areas gave the room a comfortable and inviting ambiance. Jenny's gaze wandered until it reached a long counter with a wooden live-edge top.

Behind it stood Jon, wearing jeans, a white shirt, and a black half apron. His sleeves were rolled up, and he was drying a wine glass with a kitchen towel. Billie was telling him something that made him smile.

"Here she is," Billie said when Faye and Jenny joined them at the counter.

"Hey," Faye said. She and Billie sat on either side of Jenny.

Jon set the glass down. "Hey. How are you, Faye?"

"Good."

"Hi, Jonathan," Jenny said. It was silly that she should suddenly feel shy. She was almost fifty, after all. But he really was very good-looking with that tan and those blue eyes. No wonder she used to have a crush on him.

"Hi, Jenny." He leaned on the counter and rubbed the stubble on his chin. "Long time no see, stranger."

"I know." Jenny smiled an apology. "I'm glad I'm back. I only arrived yesterday."

"I'm glad you stopped by."

"Your place is beautiful," was all Jenny could think to say.

He smiled. "I like it, too."

Jenny was out of things to say, but Jon was still looking into her eyes as if she'd just inhaled to say something more.

Jenny felt her cheeks flush warm and lowered her gaze.

She'd thrown dinners and lunches and brunches for friends and business partners and the PTA, and never once had she run out of things to say. But now, her brain was a dripping sieve, holding nothing that might help.

"We're having a welcome bonfire tonight," Billie said. "I wanted to pick up a couple of bottles of wine."

"You should come, Jon," Faye threw in.

"Let me get you something good." He turned to the shelf in the back, picked three bottles, and put them on the counter. "On the house. Welcome back, Jenny."

"You don't have to do that," she said awkwardly.

"I know." He winked. "And yet, here we are."

Jenny couldn't help but smile. "Thanks, Jon. I hope you can come to the beach tonight."

"I might, if the winery's not too busy."

"Good. Um. Bring your significant other, if you like," Jenny added.

"I'm flying solo." Jon grinned. "But I'll stop by if I can. Do you already know which beach?"

Jenny rubbed her cheek. "I don't know. Billie? What do you think?"

"The forgotten beach, of course," Billie replied. "You're going to be at the hotel tonight, won't you? Do you have plans?"

"No plans, but I should return the rental car. I'm not sure where the nearest rental place is."

"How are you going to get around without a car?" Jon asked.

Jenny shrugged. She would have to figure something out. Maybe she could pick up a used car for cheap. "The hotel is close enough to walk into Mendocino Cove."

"That's true. We used to make that trip all the time." He pulled a paper bag out from under the counter and shook it open, then put the three bonfire bottles in. Then he picked one more wine from the shelf and added it to the others. "This one's just for you. Let me know how you like it."

"You don't have to..." Jenny let her protest trail off. Obviously, Jon knew he didn't have to give her anything. She cleared her throat. "Thank you, Jon. I can't wait to taste it."

"No worries." He leaned back on the counter. "What car rental place do you need?"

Jenny told him the name of the company, and he nodded. "The nearest drop-off is in Pebble Beach. You can't walk back to Mendocino Cove. It's too far. Do you have a ride?"

"I have to do the dishes," Faye said quickly. "And Billie has a pelican wing to stretch, don't you, Billie?"

Billie hummed. "Very important for the bird to get that range of motion back. Sorry, Jenny."

"No problem. I'll just catch an Uber."

"That would work," Jon said comfortably. "Or if you don't plan on doing it until the afternoon, you can ride back with me. I have to make a trip to Pebble Beach to deliver a few boxes of wine."

"Uh. Sure. That would be great. If it's not inconvenient."

"It's not inconvenient," Jon said. "Let me give you my number."

"Okay." Jenny pulled out her phone and opened the contacts. "Here."

Jon typed his name and number and handed the phone back. "Text me so I have you in my contacts. I'll let you know when I leave for Pebble Beach."

"I will. Thanks, Jon. For the wine, too."

Billie lifted the paper bag and hopped off her chair. "Let's say seven tonight—we'll still have daylight for collecting driftwood and setting up before it gets dark."

"Thanks for the wine, Jon," Faye said and jumped off her chair too. "How is the new addition to the vineyard coming along?"

"I'm waiting to get the analysis of the soil sample. If it's in the mail today, I'll tell you all about it tonight." He hung up the towel to dry.

"Goodie. See you later, then." Faye waved and followed Billie.

"Bye, Jenny." Jon pulled off the apron.

"Thanks again, Jon. See you soon."

After she left the tasting room and before she reached the track where Faye and Billie were chatting by the open passenger door, Jenny stopped to catch a breath.

Stan had been her soulmate.

Having butterfly flutters in her stomach because Jon was maybe going to come to the bonfire was silly.

Worse, it was stupid.

She was not ten anymore. And she had enough of a mess on her hands.

CHAPTER 19

At Faye's, Jenny swapped Billie's truck for her rental and went shopping. She bought chicken, milk, a baguette and garlic butter, and eggs. On the drive back to the hotel, she beat herself up for not having peeked into the fridge the day before. It was noon and a hot day. If the fridge didn't work, her groceries would quickly go bad.

Jenny was out of the car and at the trunk to pull out her bags before she remembered how the upstairs curtain had moved. She squinted at the window. Again the cypress fanned shadow and light across the facade, but this time, the curtain hung perfectly straight. Nothing moved.

It could still have been a trick of the light.

It just wasn't likely.

Resolutely chasing away thoughts of secret squatters and wild raccoons, Jenny opened the trunk and lifted the paper bag of groceries into her arm, leaving only the paper bag with the wine. She would come back for it instead of hauling everything at once and risking dropping the bottles.

She'd not thought any more about Jon, but now her thoughts flew back to him.

It wasn't *fair* that men got more attractive with age.

"Nope," she whispered and resolutely chased away the thought of Jon's warm smile and broad shoulders too. Her situation was complicated enough. She was penniless, she was lying to the kids, and she was angry at her husband, whom she still grieved.

"All right, I'm back!" she said out loud when she pushed the old key into the lock.

Just in case someone needed a warning that she was coming in. Whether they could hear her was another question—a sea lion was barking his head off on the beach, and the gulls circling the house screamed as if they wanted chicken and wine for themselves.

Jenny stepped into the cool, blue-and-green-dappled foyer but left the door open. In the kitchen, she set her bags on the counter and opened the fridge.

"Well done, Georgie!" slipped from her lips. Whoever her aunt had hired to take care of the building had done a great job. The inside of the huge fridge was spotless and cold.

Jenny put the groceries inside, then went back to the car to fetch the wine. Again she caught herself peeking up at the window. "Nothing to see, so stop checking," she whispered to herself, hitched the bag higher in her arm, and went inside. After she put the wine in the wine rack, she went to the broom closet, got the biggest, sturdiest broom she could find, and went to the sweeping staircase leading upstairs.

She'd raised two children. She could absolutely handle squatters and raccoons.

Not spiders, though.

Jenny marched upstairs, stomping on the wide wooden stairs. When she reached the landing, she stopped. The hotel had ten spacious bedrooms, and each came with an ensuite bathroom.

"Anybody here?" she called out. "I'm coming into each room to open the windows! If anyone is in here, this is my hotel! If you leave now, I promise there will be no consequences! Don't leave, and I will call the police!" The yelling hurt her ears.

"One, two, three, four...five!" Jenny cleared her throat. "Let's do this." Gripping the broom tightly, she swung open the nearest door.

The room was empty. At least empty of people and rabid wildlife. The furniture was still there. A four-poster bed with matching nightstands and armoire, a writing desk and chair, the reading armchairs in the corner. Like ghosts, every item was covered in white drop cloth.

Jenny walked to the window and threw open the floor-length curtains. A cloud of dust rose from them. "Oof!" She coughed and waved a hand in front of her face. The window was stuck, and she had to throw her weight in before it finally flew open.

Clean, warm air streamed into the room, bringing the scent of salt and sand and cypress.

A cormorant on the roof squawked in surprise and took off. Jenny felt the whoosh from his wings as he sailed past. She leaned on the frame and looked out. There was the sea lion who had barked when she arrived. Loud as it was, it was a small animal. Jenny waved, and the sea lion lifted a flipper and waved back.

"What?" Jenny murmured and waved again. "No way."

Again, the sea lion waved back. Then it tossed its head into the neck like a prima ballerina and threw itself into the water, diving out of sight.

Jenny picked up her broom and went back into the corridor. The white coverlets on the furniture tempted her to whisk them off, but she still had to return the rental car. There was no need to look nice for the occasion, but there also was no need to cover herself in dust and cobwebs.

Leaving the door open, Jenny went to the next room. It was called the pink room. Out of childhood habit, she knocked before opening the door.

The wallpaper was even more pink than she remembered, the deep rose contrasting starkly with the white of the cloth covering the furniture. Jenny opened the curtains and the window. The sea lion resurfaced a distance from the beach, swimming back and forth.

Feeling silly, Jenny waved. This time, she got no wave in return.

One after another, Jenny went from window to window until she reached Grandma's room.

So far, the worst she had encountered was a dead, desiccated mouse. The room looking out at the driveway, where she thought the curtain had lifted, was as clean and empty as the rest.

It had been a trick of the light, after all.

Jenny put her hand on the handle of Grandma's door and paused. Rosie had been the matriarch of their little family. Her word had been law, for better or worse. Jenny closed her eyes; she felt her lips move as if they wanted to say something, but she had no words for her feelings.

Despite sending Jenny away to Nantucket to save Georgie from herself, Jenny wanted Grandma Rosie to sit in the chair by the window when she opened the door. Rosie would look up from her book and say, *You came back, Jenny. Well done, darling.*

The wish was so strong Jenny could almost hear the words echo in her head.

She could smell Grandma's scent of old lace and pipe smoke. Not only almost—the scent was real.

Her eyes flew open.

After all these years, did Grandma's room still smell like her?

Jenny opened the door and went inside.

Nothing. There was nothing, and it only smelled of dust. The furniture was covered in white; the windows were closed and hard to open. When Jenny walked back out, her gaze fell on a white urn on the dresser.

She stopped and stared at it. A faint engraving below the tapered lid read *Forever in Our Hearts.*

It was definitely an urn.

Georgie had told her she'd scattered Rosie's ashes while Jenny was at school.

Jenny hurried out of the room. This door, she closed behind her.

She skipped Mom's room entirely. She was already shaken by the urn, and if someone was hiding in her mother's room, they could stay. But the door still had the small brass plaque saying *Willow's Room* on it. Georgie had given it to her older sister as a birthday present. Jenny touched her finger to the name before she went on.

Her own room was the last one.

CHAPTER 20

For a while, Jenny stood by the door and looked at the familiar shapes. It was the only room that had no cloths draped over the furniture. Maybe by the time they made it to the last room, they'd run out.

"You have to sleep somewhere, kiddo," she finally whispered and went inside. She could pick any room, of course. But this one *belonged* to her.

The walls were still covered with posters of the '80s and her corkboard with notes and drawings and Polaroids pinned to it. Her four-poster bed was veiled by the curtains with the little stars that Mom had stitched into the sheer fabric. The bathroom had the same claw-foot tub she'd loved so much.

Jenny opened the window over the desk and leaned to look at the photos on the board. The colors had faded to sepia, but there were Faye and Billie. Their friend Ava was in one shot, and Jon in another. He stood in the background and looked at something out of frame.

She lifted the corner of the cloth on her desk. Had they found what she'd scribbled in the drawer? When she pulled it open, it was crammed full of textbooks, papers, and pencils.

Jenny had taken only what fit in Mom's two suitcases and her own book bag.

She pulled open the second drawer and found a stack of drawings. Ponies with flowing manes, houses with flower gardens, eyes with long lashes.

Grandma had kept *everything*.

She pushed the drawer shut, picked up the broom, and cleaned her room.

The next time Jenny looked at her phone, it was almost two in the afternoon. She'd missed the text from Jon, letting her know he was on his way to Pebble Beach. The rental place closed at three.

"Shoot!" She rushed back downstairs and washed her face and hands in the kitchen. Her white blouse had ended up streaked with dust after all, but there was no time to lose. Jenny grabbed an apple and her purse from the kitchen and ran outside.

The drive to Pebble Beach took half an hour. Once, Jenny got stuck behind a school bus, but she still managed to arrive in time and return the car before the place closed. When she was done, the agent walked with her to the door to lock it.

"Do you have someone to pick you up?" he asked. "I could give you a ride, but I still have to wrap up a few things."

"That's very kind of you, but I have someone I can call."

The agent nodded, satisfied, and casually flashed the peace sign. "Bye, then."

"Bye." Jenny stepped out into the sun and heard him lock up behind her. She pulled out her phone and tapped on Jon's name.

"Jenny?"

"Hi, Jon." She tugged her blouse in place. "I'm at the rental car drop-off in Pebble Beach; I just returned the car. Is your offer still good?"

"I'll meet you in a few minutes. I'm right around the corner and just about ready to leave."

"Thanks."

Jenny walked to the neighboring florist to while away the time. The window was full of gorgeous displays. She couldn't afford to splurge on flowers at the shop, but she could pick her own. The rhododendron growing by the hotel was full of pink blooms.

A truck pulled up at the curb. She turned around. The driver's door shut, and Jon came walking around the front, swinging his keys. "Hey, Jenny."

"Hey, Jon. It's good to see you." She had to blink in the afternoon sun to look up at him. She was tall, but Jon was taller. "Thank you for doing this."

"No problem. Everything okay?"

"Yep. I went shopping to stock the larder, cleaned the hotel up a bit, and returned the car." She smiled.

"Sounds like you've been busy." He opened the passenger door for her, and Jenny climbed in. "Did you have lunch?"

When Jon was seated in the driver's seat, she said, "Your sister made us such a big breakfast this morning; I haven't been hungry since. I do look forward to the bonfire, though."

"I do, too." Jon started the truck and pulled into the road. "We don't do those often enough. Everyone's busy."

"I know." Jenny looked out the window. "It's strange that beach fires are still allowed. I was sure they had become a thing of the past."

"It's still allowed on some beaches." They talked about the wildfires and the beaches until Jon flicked the blinker and turned into Mendocino Cove. The forgotten beach was just inside the town lines; the village, the historic heart of Mendocino Cove, was another ten minutes away.

"Can I bring anything tonight?" Jon asked.

"You already contributed the wine," she reminded him. "I bought chicken to grill, and Faye said she was going to bring foil potatoes."

Jon slowed the truck and turned into Forgotten. "I have not been here since you left," he said when he stopped in front of the hotel.

Jenny jumped out. "It's that kind of place," she said and smiled at him. "Thanks so much for the ride, Jon. I'm glad you can make it tonight."

Jon smiled back.

Jenny closed the door and waved, watching Jon turn around and drive back up the lane. She went to one of the flowering rhododendrons and took a selfie of herself in front of it. Then she clipped off a few of the purple blooms and went into the house to text the selfie to her kids.

Audrey wrote back right away with lots of questions about Jenny's trip, and Jenny did her best to field them while putting the flowers in vases.

When are you coming back?

Jenny stopped to think about what she should say. *Not sure. Might sell the house in Portland*, she texted finally. *It's beautiful here.*

Hang in there, Mom, Audrey texted back. *Don't worry. And don't do anything rash.*

Jenny tilted her head. That didn't exactly sound as if she had convinced Audrey that all was well.

Another text dinged, and she opened it.

We're coming over now, Billie informed her. *Collect wood before dark.*

Jenny checked the time. *Okay*, she texted Billie, and to Audrey, *You hang in there yourself. Why aren't you asleep??*

Then she set the phone down and got chicken, onions, and mushrooms from the fridge. The least she could do as a thank-you to her old friends was make kebabs for dinner.

They still had an hour before starting the fire. Jenny hummed, grateful the girls were coming over early.

CHAPTER 21

Faye set her load on the counter in the hotel kitchen and shook out her arms. "I brought a few things to eat."

Jenny's eyes widened when she saw the bulging bags. "How many people did you two invite?"

"It's only us and Jon." Billie added a couple of totes of her own. "Faye, I didn't know you were going to get stuff too."

"I didn't know *you* would stop by the market. I guess great minds think alike." Faye grinned.

Unlike the day before, the hotel had woken up. The mood was good. As if the old house liked having its doors and windows thrown open and vases with flowers scattered throughout, the atmosphere had gone from spooky-dusty to airy-happy overnight. "I thought for sure you'd be busy force-feeding pelicans," Faye said to Billie.

"It's one pelican, Faye." Billie started to unpack. "And he eats everything he can get his hands on. Or his beak, rather. Zero force-feeding required."

"How is his wing?" Jenny intercepted mildly.

"Good! A few more days and he'll be fine. I can't wait to release him. Neither can he." Outside, the sea lion barked. Billie tilted her head.

"That one." Jenny spread her palms wide on the counter. "It's only one little sea lion out front, but he's as loud as an entire herd."

"That bark sounds familiar." Billie went to the window.

Faye joined her. "I think that's a tag on the tail, Billie, isn't it?"

Billie raised on her tiptoes. "Polly?" she yelled out of the window.

The sea lion barked back and waved a flipper.

Jenny joined them. "Did you *raise* it?"

"Her. Polly's my little girl." Billie narrowed her eyes. "She's not supposed to be here."

"I thought you didn't let them get used to humans."

"*I* don't." Exasperated, Billie shook her head. "Whatever went wrong with her imprinting wasn't my fault."

"So she just likes humans?"

"Since before she came to me. I'm pretty sure someone befriended her. Maybe she was even raised with a bottle."

"Aww. I can't be mad."

"I worry about her," Billie said. "When I got her, she was injured."

"Was it a shark?" Jenny asked.

"It looked like she got too close to the propeller of a fishing boat motor," Billie replied. "Maybe I was wrong to release her again. Being too trusting can be a big problem for a wild animal."

"She looks great, Billie," Faye said. "Healthy and happy. You did the right thing."

"She was in the cove yesterday," Jenny said. "This morning, she waved at me. I thought I was crazy."

"Don't encourage her," Billie said bossily.

"I can't wave?"

"You can wave. But don't feed or touch her."

"She finds plenty of food on her own," Faye commented. Polly had a plump layer of blubber. "Maybe she just wants company."

"Nooo," Billie murmured. "Go find yourself a nice herd to hang out with, Polly."

"Poor thing." Jenny knew how it felt to be a lonely orphan. "She and I can be friends at a distance. I'll wave when I see her."

Billie sighed and returned to the counter.

Faye joined her and patted her shoulder. "There, there," she murmured.

Jenny resumed slicing chicken breasts. "I'm making kebabs," she announced. "I found a bag of barbecue charcoal in the shed and dug out the old fire ring. The grill grid is gone, but we can use an oven rack."

"I brought aluminum foil." Billie pulled two long blue boxes from her bag. "And everything we need for making charred corn on the cob with chili powder and lime juice." She lifted the ingredients from the tote one by one. "Also grilled sweet potatoes with feta cheese and salmon filets with dill. I'm in a healthy mood today."

"Okay." Jenny sounded impressed. "Great!"

"I got skewered shrimp marinated in lime and garlic and marinated steak." Faye added her packages to Billie's pile. "Goes well with the charred corn, too."

"Shrimp and steak too?" Jenny put down her knife.

"And cornbread muffins with a green chili and cheese filling." Faye crumpled up the empty paper bag for the fire. "Since this is a welcome back party, I thought we should be fancy and make appetizers and dessert."

"Dessert?" Billie pulled the second bag over for a glimpse. "What do we get? Fresh fruit?" She took out a small bunch of bananas.

"Grilled bananas with marshmallows and walnuts and chocolate sauce," Faye corrected her. "Plus, pineapple slices wrapped in prosciutto for appetizers. I usually use bacon, but we already ate bacon for breakfast. I'll grill the pineapple first, wrap it in prosciutto, and grill just for a moment longer. I have a whole plan."

Jenny frowned at her humble chicken. "Here I thought chicken and mushroom kebabs were enough."

"It's always good to have leftovers." Billie lifted an eyebrow at Faye.

"I agree," Faye said quickly. Neither she nor Billie knew how much money Jenny had for frivolous dinners or how long her money would have to last her. Chipping in with the beach party dinner had been a no-brainer, but maybe they should've told Jenny they'd take care of the food. "Come on, let's get everything ready. I'm starving, and we haven't even started building the fire yet."

"Go ahead." Billie got off her stool and stretched. "I'm going to chase Polly off the beach and gather driftwood." She strode out of the kitchen.

"That I want to see." Faye set the package of shrimp in the sink and went back to the window. "Jenny, come have a look."

It wasn't long before Billie appeared in view. "Shoo! Shoo!" she yelled. "Git, Polly!"

Polly barked and started galloping, sea lion style, toward Billie.

"No!" Billie waved her hands to scare Polly away. "Go! Go find other sea lions!"

Polly stopped. She weaved her head from side to side as if she was doing a silly trick.

"Oh well." Faye chuckled. "At least Billie can say she tried."

Polly resumed a steady march toward Billie, who kept yelling for her to go away. Eventually, the sea lion reached her former caretaker and started rubbing her head on Billie's jeans.

"No!" Billie backed away. "Bad Polly!"

The sea lion threw back her sleek head and barked a laugh, then turned, waddled to the water, and threw herself in the waves.

Billie watched for a moment, then started to pick up the dry driftwood that was abundantly scattered in the sand.

When the shrimp and chicken were cleaned and marinated, the corn chucked, and the potatoes wrapped, they put everything in the fridge and decided to go outside.

Faye tried to stay tuned to the good energy of the kitchen as she went through the living room. The room was flooded with sun, the long curtains tied back. Jenny had dusted the tables and shelves and put out vases with bright pink, purple, and white rhododendron blossoms. Despite the old-fashioned fabrics, the large room looked bright and beautiful, merging seamlessly into the beach.

Faye passed the grand piano, and just for that moment, it felt as if a mute sigh wavered in the air, a look from hidden eyes followed her, a touch without fingers raised the hairs on her neck.

"Brrr." She shivered and hurried outside, where the sand was warm and grounding.

"You all right, Faye?" Jenny stepped out behind her. "Was that another piece of seaweed touching you?"

"Not seaweed." Faye rubbed her neck and glanced an apology at her friend. "Just my imagination."

"Yeah?" Jenny looked back over her shoulder into the living room. "I hope you didn't walk through a cobweb. I can't handle spiders."

"I'm fine with spiders," Faye murmured automatically. "It's the—" She broke off just in time.

"The what?" Jenny had caught it. "What?"

Faye did not want to say anything, but then she took a breath. Jenny was her friend, after all. "The *energy*," she said and smiled an apology.

"What energy? Electricity?"

"Yes, but not the electricity from a power outlet. The energy in the air. It's like a sudden buzz."

"Our little Faye has grown up to be a psychic," Billie mentioned as she passed them to dump a load of wood by the grill before going to get more.

"Ah," Jenny said. "Your psychic ability is picking up on something in the hotel?"

There was no sarcasm in her friend's voice. "I didn't feel it in the kitchen. It's in the living room. Almost like a little pinch," Faye said.

"A pinch?" Jenny's eyebrow rose. "Do I have a ghost pinching people?"

Faye smiled. "Maybe. Or I'm imagining things. That's possible too."

Jenny ignored this second, more likely option. "You feel this as soon as you enter the room?"

It hadn't been until—"When I passed the piano," Faye said.

Billie had amassed a pile of wood and joined them, rubbing sand off her hands. "What about the piano?" she wanted to know.

"Faye feels a ghostly pinch when she passes it," Jenny explained.

"Oh." Billie's eyes widened. "Yesterday's seaweed all over again, huh? That was by the piano too."

"Yes, exactly. It's the seaweed thing all over again."

"We need to do a séance." Billie chuckled. "Like they did back in the olden days. Someone to rattle the table with their knee and pull a string to open the chest of drawers."

"Maybe we should," Faye said and touched her neck. The little hairs at the base of her skull were still standing up. "Maybe we should have a séance."

"I don't know." Jenny shaded her eyes from the sinking sun and looked into the living room. "Guys, don't freak me out. I want to sleep in my old bedroom tonight."

"You can always come stay with me," Billie offered.

"I think...well, let's not do a full-blown séance," Faye said. "Let's just go inside and listen."

Jenny rubbed her arm. "What if there *is* a ghost and we hear something?"

"Then you'll stay with Billie and me instead of alone in the Forgotten Cove," Faye said. "Let's go stand by the piano and hold hands and close our eyes and listen."

Billie pinched the bridge of her nose, then sighed and looked up. "Did you check for raccoons, Jen?"

"None that I could find," Jenny said.

"Right." Billie strode to the hotel. "Come on, you two. Let's settle this ghostly seaweed business once and for all."

Faye shrugged. "Better now than in the dead of night, right?"

Jenny swallowed. "I'm not closing my eyes, though."

"You *have* to."

CHAPTER 22

O kay." Jenny put a hand on the piano. She ran a cloth over it earlier, but the wood that used to gleam warm and rich was far from polished. "I don't feel anything. No seaweed, no buzzing. Faye?"

"Uh. I'm not...no." Faye shrugged her shoulders.

"You look like someone is tickling your neck," Billie said. "What do we do?"

"I have no idea." Faye held out her hands. "Let's sit with it."

"Do we have to hold hands to sit with it?" Billie eyed Faye's hands as if she suspected a trick.

Jenny laughed. "Oh, come on, Bills. This is just like way back when we were eight." She took one of Faye's hands and held out her other.

Hesitantly, Billie took it. "Uh. I don't know. This is silly. Besides..."

"Besides...what?" Faye asked.

"Besides, maybe it's better not to stir anything up." Billie coughed, looking embarrassed. "I mean, just in case."

"In case ghosts are real?" Faye's eyes glittered with amusement.

"Of course they're not real. It's just in case. Full stop."

"That makes no sense, Billie," Jenny said reasonably. "It's an either-or situation. Either they are real, or they're not."

"That's right." Faye wiggled her fingers. "You don't believe in any of this. Let's just do it so Jenny can sleep in peace."

"Why do I let you boss me around?" Billie took Faye's hand and closed the circle.

"You can't resist my animal magnetism." Faye giggled, but it sounded thin and nervous. "Wait. I'm going to close the curtain. It's too bright for ghosts in here."

"Aww, come *on*," Billie moaned. "I came for a bonfire and grilled corn, not to stand around dark Victorian parlors and hold sweaty hands. No offense, Jenny."

"It's not a parlor," Jenny said. "It's the living room. And my hands are dry. I don't want to wake up tonight wondering whether that's seaweed touching my face." She went to help Faye untie the curtains. She didn't believe in ghosts, either. But like Billie, Jenny had a tiny corner in her head where two words followed each other in a never-ending loop. *What if,* they whispered. *What if, what if, what if...*

"Hear our girl, Billie? She doesn't want to wake up wondering." Faye pulled the curtain closed across the open doors. They billowed outward, flapping like albatross wings.

"Eerie," Jenny said. "Maybe I'll take you up on your offer to couch-crash after all, Billie."

"You're welcome anytime." Billie shook her head. "I'm giving this five minutes, Faye. No longer."

They took each other's hands. Jenny felt silly and a bit nervous. She gripped Billie's hand harder.

"Close your eyes. Think of... I don't know. Ghosts? No—just *feel* the room."

"Feel the *room?*" Billie closed her eyes. "How does one—"

"Billie, shush." Faye, too, closed her eyes. "Concentrate. Focus."

"On what?" Billie murmured.

It wasn't dark in the room, but the curtains blocked the bright evening sun, creating a dim, misty light.

"Are your eyes closed, Jenny?" Faye asked.

"Yes." Jenny closed her eyes.

"*Feel*," Faye murmured.

"But *what?*" Billie whispered again.

They were quiet.

At first, closing her eyes made Jenny dizzy. As if she would fall any moment. She focused on the feel of Faye's hand and Billie's holding her own. Faye's fingers were warm, and Billie's were cold, as if the two represented opposite poles. Slowly, the dizziness faded.

With the curtains keeping the breeze out, the air in the room grew warmer.

Jenny lowered her hunched shoulders. Nothing was happening. She couldn't feel anything but cold fingers and warm ones. Suddenly, a wave of relaxation went through Jenny. Warm, warm, it was as warm as if someone was holding her in their arms, as if Mom was cradling her again. She lay curled in her mother's embrace. Her arms held her tight, her face was hidden...hidden.

A loud bang startled Jenny. "Ah!" Her eyes flew open.

Faye and Billie shrieked too, pulling their hands back.

Bright light flicked on. "What the—"

"*Jon!*" Billie yelled. "What are you doing here? You scared us to death!"

They stared at Jon, their hearts pumping and their legs shaking, and Jon, hand on the light switch, stared back.

Then he started laughing. "What am *I* doing? What are *you* doing? Are you nuts?"

"It's not funny!" Billie put her hands on her knees to catch her breath. "Have you heard of knocking?"

"I did! I did knock!" Jon gestured at the foyer. "I thought you were on the beach and couldn't hear me. I didn't know you were...standing in a circle..." He laughed again.

Jenny's heart was still beating in her throat, but she had to give it to Jon. Three middle-aged women holding hands in a dark room was pretty nuts.

"We were conjuring Jenny's ghost." Irritated, Faye shook her hair back.

Jon stopped chuckling. "Jenny has a ghost?"

"I don't exactly *know* that I do," Jenny said and smiled at him. "We got spooked and wanted to check, I guess. It lives near the piano. We think."

After a short silence, Jon asked, "Are you all done?"

"Yes," Faye announced. "We're done."

Jon pointed at the curtains. "Can we open those, please?"

"Sure." Jenny went to pull them aside. The sun was sinking, and the last golden rays, tinged pink and red, fell into the room like fiery garlands. She blinked.

"Okay. Uh." Faye rubbed her eyes. "Anyways. What's the verdict, ladies?"

"You tell us," Billie said. "Did you feel anything?"

"Feel what, exactly?" Jon asked, interested.

"The ghostly presence," Billie said.

"No." Faye shook her head. "All I could think about was that we should go outside."

"Sounds reasonable," Jon said. "It is a beautiful evening out there. What did you feel, Billie?" He grinned at his sister.

"I felt cold," Billie said. "Let's start the bonfire and the grill too. Brrr."

"Funny," Jenny said. "I was really warm. Like I was taking a bath."

"There you have it." Jon nodded, satisfied. "Everyone feels something different. Nice and normal. No ghosts."

"Yeah." Faye looked over her shoulder. "Uh, Jen?"

"What?"

Faye pointed at the old armoire that stood between the piano and the wall. "Did you open the doors? I know for a fact it was closed when we came into the room."

"I didn't touch it."

"Oh no!" Billie whimpered.

"Oh, come on." Jon went to the armoire and opened it all the way. "It's old wood. The doors probably flap open and shut all the time in the draft."

Jenny came to look too. "I think Grandma used to store her tablecloths here."

"It looks like your grandma repurposed it while you were gone." Jon stepped aside so Jenny could see.

CHAPTER 23

The armoire was stuffed full of boxes and cartons, quilts and linen, and papers. Jenny took a tiny pink paper box from the top shelf and pried it open, taking out the square of fabric inside and shaking it out. "What's this?"

"That's a handkerchief," Jon said evenly. "And the things stitched in the corner are little flowers."

She almost elbowed him. "Thank you for mansplaining."

"Hey, you asked." He picked out another small box and opened it. "A pocket watch—wow. It's heavy." He lifted out the silver watch on a chain. "There is a ship engraved on the back. Is it your grandpa's?"

"Could be. It looks valuable." Jenny folded the handkerchief back into the same folds and returned it to the armoire. Had Grandma stitched it for her trousseau as a young woman? She picked another box. Unlike Jon's, this one was red velvet and bigger. She wiggled off the lid, curious.

"What's this? A miniature?" She lifted it out. "It's a carousel." Tiny carved boats followed each other in a circle. In the middle stood a palm tree painted in faded pastels.

"Look, there's a tiny little key taped to the bottom." Faye pointed. "It's a music box."

"Does it still work?" Jenny tried the key. It fit in the lock on the bottom. She turned it and let go. A sweet melody whirred, and the carousel of boats turned, each going up and down as if it was riding the waves of an ocean.

"That's cute—I bet you I could sell it for a small fortune." Faye wiggled between Jon and Jenny and reached for her own box. The red wood had faded to lavender pink. She wiggled the lid off. "Oh. Oh."

"What is it?"

Faye exhaled audibly and lifted out a thin rectangle with a colorful design on it. "Unless I'm mistaken, this is a set of antique ivory playing cards. Jenny, these sell for a small fortune. Where does all this treasure come from?"

"I have no idea." Jenny took a card from Faye and studied it. "I've never seen this in my life. It's beautiful. Like something that should be in a museum."

"Better put it back."

Jenny did as she was told, and Faye carefully closed the lid again. Then she set it back. "We shouldn't just unbox these things on the fly. Jenny, you do it when you have time. Meanwhile, I recommend locking the armoire."

Jenny couldn't remember whether the armoire even had a key. "I'll have a look later," she promised.

"Are these your grandpa's things, Jen?" Billie peered over Faye's shoulder.

"I don't know. He died when I was four. It might be his. Though now it belongs to my aunt."

"Does she know what's in the armoire?" Billie asked.

"It's very hard to say what Georgie knows and doesn't know," Jenny said. "But I will tell her next time we talk. I can take photos and see if she at least wants to appraise and insure some of the stuff. The hotel isn't exactly hard to break into."

She was about to close the doors when something caught her eye.

"I recognize this quilt." Jenny pulled the folded quilt out. "It used to be on Mom's bed."

She let the quilt fall open. All the patches had nature motives, and Jenny remembered each one. "Mom loved it," she said quietly. "Grandma stitched the images on the fabric herself." There was a tree, a fern, a moon and a star, several intricate flowers, the sea and the beach.

Grandma had made it for Mom's tenth birthday, and Mom had never stopped using it. Jenny brought it outside and hung it over a cypress branch to air out. It could keep her warm tonight.

"What's on the second shelf?" Faye pulled out a flat case that looked like an attaché case and handed it to Jenny. "I think I know," she said. "Open it."

Jenny flicked open the little locks and lifted the lid. "Oh," she said. "It's our good silverware."

"Hotel silver," Faye agreed. "It's tarnished, but you can polish it. It might be worth something if you need cash."

"Well, it also belongs to Aunt Georgie." Jenny closed the lid again. "I might steal my mother's old quilt, but I draw the line at the family silver."

"It's a shelf full of heirlooms," Billie said suddenly. "All those little things, the quilts, silver, and look, those are photo albums."

"Here." Jon handed Jenny a bulky album. She flipped it open.

There was a young Rosie standing on the beach in a blue-and-white belted Seersucker dress, looking like she belonged to Nantucket, not Mendocino Cove. Beside her stood Grandpa as a young man, with his bronzed face and black hair and white teeth. The two were holding hands and smiling at each other.

"That must be your mom." Faye pointed at the chubby baby sitting on a towel between them.

"That's her," Jenny confirmed. "And the lady sitting in the chair here is my great-grandmother, Magda. She was ninety-five years old when I was born. Apparently, I spent most of my first year of life in her arms. She passed away shortly after I turned two." She smiled fondly. "Grandma used to tell me that I looked like the spitting image of Magda. What do you think?"

"If you think away the wrinkles, you do." Faye leaned in to see better. "It's almost eerie. Your eyes are exactly the same." She hugged herself. "Do you remember her?"

"I have a lovely memory of an old woman smiling down at me. It's just a single image of a smiling, wrinkly face with bright eyes. But I believe it is Magda."

"It could be. Two years is awfully young for remembering anything."

"It's hard to tell apart what's real and what's imagination," Jenny admitted. "Grandma often talked about her mother, and of course I know Magda loved me even though our lives only overlapped for a short time." Jenny frowned. "I would love to have these photos. The salty air in the hotel can't be good for them."

Gently, Jon took the album from Jenny and set it back. Then he closed the door. "The photos are fine in those plastic pockets. For now...I'm starving, and I've had enough of ghosts and memories. Let's make a fire before the sun sinks."

He put one hand on Jenny's shoulder and one on Billie's, gently turning them so they faced the beach. "Twilight is not the time to look at faded photos of lost loved ones. That's best done early in the morning, over strong coffee and chocolate croissants and birds singing in front of the window."

"You're right," Billie said, relief in her voice. "This *is* supposed to be a party. We've done enough spooky stuff for the evening. It's time to eat."

"Agreed," Jenny said. The beach was calling her, too. She could have a look at the other things in the armoire tomorrow morning if she felt like it. It wasn't always necessary to dig up the past.

"Where did you say you saw the charcoal for the grill, Jen?" Faye asked.

"I already brought everything to the barbeque pit outside. Let me go get a lighter."

"I have matches on me." Billie produced a small box from the pocket of her jeans. "I'll help you start the grill, Faye."

The two marched off, jumping as far as they could from the open door into the sand and laughing about it.

"Jenny?" Jon asked in a low voice. "Do you have a minute?"

Now Jenny knew what Faye meant by a buzzing feeling on her skin. "What's up?"

"Can I show you something out front?" He nodded his head toward the foyer.

"Okay." Jenny followed, although she'd rather have joined the girls. Her life was already complicated. Childhood crush throwbacks didn't help.

Jon opened the front door and pointed. Leaning against his pickup truck was a bicycle.

"Whoa. What's this?" It looked like a carbon copy of the bike Jenny used to have as a teen. The frame was bright blue, had a wicker basket in the front, and a rack to seat friends in the back. They all used to have bikes, to go where they wanted without having to ask for a rarely granted car ride.

"Now that you don't have a car anymore," Jon said, "I thought you could use this."

"Really? It's so pretty." Jenny was having a major déjà vu moment. She walked over and touched the bike. "You didn't buy this for me, did you?"

Jon ran a hand through his hair. "I bought it for...well, never mind. I've had it for a while."

"Because it looks new." Jenny looked up.

"It's not, actually."

"It looks like a bike I used to have."

"I know." Again, Jon ran his hand through his hair. "I liked the color of that bike."

Jenny turned to him. "You did?"

"I did." He looked back at her, straight into her eyes. "I liked seeing that flash of blue come around the corner more than anything. I still do."

Jenny smiled. She grabbed the handlebars and pulled the bike toward her, tempted to swing her leg over the saddle and ride into the sunset. She looked back at him, squinting into the last glow of the sun behind him. "And, uh...did you like Faye's bike as well?" she asked casually.

"*Faye?*" He grinned. "Faye's bike was green, Jen. I've always been more of a blue kind of guy." He raised a single eyebrow, blatantly flirting now.

Jenny chuckled. Whether she liked it or not, he was still as cute as she remembered. "I see."

"Yeah." He crossed his arms in front of his chest, looked at his feet and back at her, and then he laughed. "So, what, can you use it? It's hogging garage space I need for my more manly bikes."

"I would love to borrow it while I'm here," Jenny said. "Though to be honest, I haven't biked in years."

"Well, it's like, you know—*riding a bike*. You don't forget how to do it." Jon watched her play with the brake handle and the shiny golden bell.

"Sure. I'll figure it out. It will be so useful for getting around." Jenny wheeled the bike over to the house and propped it against a low, smooth cypress branch.

"Thanks very much, Jon." She went to him and touched his arm, and before she could think better of it, raised on tiptoes and kissed Jon's cheek. "That was very thoughtful of you. I appreciate it."

"You're...very welcome. Uh, I'm... You're welcome, Jenny." He rubbed a hand over his chin, the fingertips touching the spot she had kissed.

"Should we go back?" Jenny pointed a thumb over her shoulder at the door. "The grill is probably ready for some food."

"Yes." Jon followed her into the kitchen, where they took the prepared food out of the fridge and carried it outside to the barbecue.

CHAPTER 24

T here they are! Here." Billie handed them each a glass of white wine, hooked her arm under her brother's, and dragged him off to light the bonfire.

"Everything okay?" Faye came to stand by Jenny's side.

"Jon just gave me a bike," Jenny said and took a long drink. "I mean, it's a loan. But the bike looks exactly like the one I used to have."

"I'm pretty sure it's a gift, not a loan." Faye smiled. "It *is* your bike, you know? He asked Rosie if he could buy it ages ago."

Jenny lowered her glass. "Are you serious?"

"He put a lot of work into making it as good as new." Faye bit her lip. "Don't tell him I told you."

"Oh." Jenny didn't know what to make of that information. "Uh, no. I won't."

"All of us struggled when you moved to the East Coast. Fixing the bike was his way of staying close to you. Kind of romantic, don't you think?"

"Romantic?" Jenny glanced at Faye. There was an impish glint in her friend's eyes that she remembered only too well.

"You always did have a crush on him." Faye lifted her glass to cheer Jenny. "As a little schoolgirl, I mean."

"Ah, shucks. How did you know?" Smiling, Jenny cheered back and drank. Raising her kids had taught her how obvious teens could be. Especially when they thought they were keeping deep, dark secrets.

"*Everyone* knew." Faye picked up the bottle that was standing on a log of driftwood and refilled Jenny's glass. "Everyone except Jon."

Jenny shook her head. "I thought it was hopeless."

Down at the water, Jon was chasing Billie with a long strip of kelp. Billie, after unsuccessfully swatting back at her brother, was laughing so hard she stumbled and fell into the sand.

"Nah." Faye patted Jenny's arm. "You should have said something. His crush on you was even worse."

"Jon had a crush on me?" Jenny pulled her chin back. "He barely even looked at me."

"Yeah well, there are no classes teaching the graceful handling of crushes, are there? We didn't even have the internet. None of us knew how to do *anything*."

Jenny took another sip. "I'm not so sure you're right." Jon would have let her know. Something, somehow. It would have been so easy.

"Hand me the shrimp." Faye adjusted the oven rack on the stones and covered it with foil to make a cooking surface. Jenny handed her the marinated shrimp, and Faye laid them head to tail on the foil.

"When you left," Faye said after a while, "that was pretty sudden. For you most of all, of course. But for us, too. One day we were tighter than sisters. The next day, you were gone."

"It was hard." Jenny exhaled. She didn't like to think back to that time.

When Mom first went missing, the stress had been unbearable. Time turned into a blur of danger. Sleep became the enemy. Food was dust and ash. Friends, even sisters of the heart, didn't matter because their life wasn't in danger.

It took the forest rangers two weeks to find her. She was miles off the trail, curled under the exposed root of a fallen fir in her shorts and T-shirt and birding binoculars.

"It was hard," she repeated quietly. Her world had ended as she stood in the door of the kitchen, kneading her fingers, watching with terror in her heart as Grandma cried, unable to say the words Jenny was dreading to hear.

"You lost your mom in such a terrible way."

"I was a mess," Jenny admitted. "But Aunt Georgie *lost* it. She kept going into the forest as if she could bring Mom back. Grandma was scared for her, so she talked Georgie into moving to Nantucket. Grandma said we used to have family on the island, and Georgie had always wanted to go."

"We were told Georgie took *you* to Nantucket for a new beginning and a chance to heal."

"That was the other part of it. We took each other, I suppose."

"How did that work out? Did you track down your family there?"

"Nobody shared my great-grandmother Magda's surname, and I don't have any names from before that. I even asked Grandma, but she drew a blank too."

"Bummer."

"The kinship would have been diluted quite a lot, anyway." Jenny smiled. "It's not like you can walk up to someone and be like, hey, I think we are relatives to the fifth degree."

"I guess that would be weird. I did one of those DNA test kits that alerts you to relatives. Relatives with heavy air quotes, that is. I ignore anyone who is not at least a second cousin. Anyway. Did you at least like it there?"

"We did. Nantucket is beautiful, and we needed the change. It was different enough from Mendocino Cove, but there were enough similarities to make the homesickness bearable." Jenny had figured the soft, unsettled feeling of not belonging was simply part of being an adult. Like taxes and car repairs. "I only moved because Stan wanted to be closer to his parents in Portland."

"I wish you could have stayed with my family," Faye said. "Mom even asked, but of course Rosie wanted you to be with Georgie." She turned the shrimp to grill the other side. "Even back then, I understood that was the way it had to be. But I didn't like it."

"Georgie would have gone mad here," Jenny confirmed. "Moving to Nantucket saved her life. Or at least her sanity, such as it is. I had no energy left to rebel, but I wonder what my life would have been had I stayed."

"Meanwhile, I wonder what my life would have been had I *left*," Faye said and smiled. "Let's not worry about the what-ifs and could've-beens. It won't change anything. I'm sure Nantucket and Portland are beautiful, and I can't complain about Mendocino, either."

Jenny picked up a shrimp by the tail. Her appetite had returned. She blew to cool it, then took a bite. "Grandma should have come with us," she said before remembering they were done with the whats and ifs.

Faye flipped the food once more. A drop fell and hissed on the hot coals. "She told Mom it was too late for her to start over. She couldn't leave the memories behind."

"She said that?" Jenny pressed her lips together. "I figured it was the case, but why didn't she tell me?"

"Mom was a friend stopping by for a cup of tea and a chat. I'm sure Rosie treated you differently. She wanted you to start over, not worry about her."

"Mh-mm." Jenny scratched her shoulder. She knew a thing or two about pretending everything was fine so the kids had peace of mind. After all, she was lying to her kids. Since she'd shielded Georgie as best she could, maybe it had become a habit long before she had River. But was it effective? Audrey's texts suggested her daughter at least wasn't buying the vacation story.

Jenny cleared her throat. "Still, being all alone here..." She knew she should change the topic instead of roping Faye any deeper into the topic. At the same time, the words wanted out. They needed air and light; they needed the ear and understanding of a friend. "It must have been terribly lonely. Georgie tried for years to get Grandma to join us."

"Ha," Faye said, and she actually sounded amused. "Rosie was as stubborn as a manatee."

"You can say that again. She never even listened to Georgie, just started to talk over her. And if *I* brought it up, she would just hang up on me."

"I only caught little bits of information here and there," Faye said. "None of it was meant for my ears, either."

"How was Grandma?" Jenny couldn't help but stare at her friend, unable to look away in case she would lose the smallest trace of information. For so many years, she'd wondered how Grandma had really lived out her life.

"Oh, Jen." Faye smiled at her. "Don't worry. Rosie lived alone, but she sure wasn't lonely. Mom went over to have tea all the time, and so did a few other women in town. Rosie wasn't always happy to see them, either. She liked to sit on the beach by herself, smoking her pipe and looking out at the ocean."

That sounded familiar. Jenny liked to do the same thing, minus the smoking. "I was afraid everyone would forget about the cove, and Grandma in it."

"Oh, please." Faye grinned. "The cove was so full of Rosie; people didn't have a chance to forget it. Even when she had one of her solitary fits, my mom would sneak around the house and leave casseroles on the beach for Rosie. Then Rosie would call our house, all mad, saying she was perfectly able to cook her own casseroles and leaving food on the beach only attracted the cormorants." Faye took a loaf of baguette filled with garlic butter and set it on the grill.

"I wish I could give your mom a hug," Jenny said. "I wouldn't have worried so much had I known about this."

"Mom told Georgie. She probably should have let you know instead." Faye put the shrimp on a platter and straightened. "Look, Jenny. They got the fire going."

The first bonfire flames crackled over the pile of dry beach wood. Billie and Jon were standing by, drinking wine.

"Let's eat the shrimp while we cook the rest." Faye expertly arranged the corn and sweet potatoes filled with feta cheese near the flames, pushing the chicken to the side so it wouldn't burn.

"Billie! Jon! You want shrimp and garlic bread?" Jenny called out. The siblings turned and waved. Jenny filled plates and brought them to the bonfire.

"I almost forgot, but I brought a cooler with some food too. It's in the truck," Jon said. "Hang on." He popped a shrimp in his mouth and jogged off, barefoot, the hem of his rolled-up jeans wet with sea spray.

"Here." Jenny handed Billie a plate. "Enjoy."

They sat on one of the logs Jon had dragged over. There were three in total, one on each side of the fire, leaving the view to the sea open.

"Those sunsets. I can't get enough of them." Jenny marveled at the bright reds blooming in the sky and spilling into the sea. "I spent three decades in a place where sun and sea don't kiss good night."

"It's very important they do." Billie bit into a shrimp. "These are great. Well done, Faye."

"Good." Faye joined them, climbing over the log with a plate in one hand and a glass of wine in the other.

"They really are delicious." Jenny chewed happily. Guarded by rocks and sand, the bonfire crackled and sparked into the falling dark. The sweet scent of burning driftwood mingled with the aroma of sun-dried kelp. Polly sat in the shallow surf like a plump shadow, grunting contentedly.

"Can Polly have grilled shrimp?" Jenny asked.

"Oh my goodness! No." Billie drank wine and shook her head at the same time, and when she coughed, Jenny and Faye laughed.

"I'm just teasing you," Jenny promised and ate the snack herself.

"Here comes more food." Jon appeared beside her, his footsteps swallowed by the soft sand. He set down an enormous ice chest.

"Oh." Jenny put her glass to the other side so he could step over the log and sit beside her. "What's in it?"

"Whatever it is, there'll be a lot of it." Faye craned her neck to see. "The Donovans go all in when they cook."

"It's how we relax." Jon lifted out trays of finger foods, peeling off the protective foil as he set them on top of the cooler. "Empanadas with a tangy cream sauce, crab cakes with remoulade, cheese quesadillas with a tomato-basil dip—"

"You made my favorite!" Faye reached a long arm across Jenny to scoop up a handful of the bite-sized crab cakes.

"—fruit skewers with pineapple, watermelon, mango, and mint," Jon finished. "Also, iced tea and lemonade. Those are in the cooler."

"Whoa." Jenny was impressed. "That's a lot."

"We grew up in extended families that like to eat. It feels weird not to make too much," Billie confirmed. "Try Jon's crab cakes. They're unbelievable."

Jon offered the tray with its neat rows of cakes. "Secret family recipe."

"Really?"

He winked. "No. I found it on the internet. It had two thousand five-star ratings."

"Either way—don't mind if I do." Jenny piled two cakes as well as samples of the other foods on her plate.

Jon went around to offer the trays to Faye and his sister. Faye got up to get the last food from the grill and refill their wine glasses, Billie stoked the fire, and everyone ordered Jenny to sit back and relax.

The sun dove into the Pacific, and a golden moon rose. Jenny rolled up her jeans and stepped to her ankles into the cool, dark water. She snapped a picture of the moonshine on the waves for the kids, and when Faye started singing in a high, sweet voice into the night and Polly rumbled a harmony, Jenny thought that even though she had no money and the future was uncertain, this was the happiest she had been in months.

CHAPTER 25

"Hey, Jon. Are you working? Is that why I haven't seen you in ages?" Billie pressed a kiss on her brother's head, then sank with a grateful sigh on a stool and put her purse on the old wine barrel that served as a table.

It was dinnertime, and the doors to the tasting room were wide open. The evening sun lit up the vineyard, casting the valleys in soft shadows and illuminating the golden tops of the rolling hills. The tables quickly filled with guests.

"Hey, Billie. I do have to work sometimes," Jon said mildly and closed his laptop. "Besides, what do you mean, long time? We saw each other last night at the bonfire." He got up to bring Billie a glass of her favorite white wine spritzer before sitting down again. "Rough day at the office?"

"A sport fisher brought in a cormorant," Billie reported. "She's terribly underweight, but I have no idea why."

"Can you save her?"

"She ate. A lot. Cross your fingers that it sticks to her ribs." Billie took a sip of the cold drink. "Mmm."

"Hannah brought the food truck over," Jon said and nodded at his empty plate. "I might go for seconds. Does Michael realize how good a cook she is? Her talent is wasted working as a waitress at the Mermaid Galley."

"Michael doesn't even realize she has a food truck." Billie smiled. "I'd sure like to be there when he finds out. What's on the menu tonight?"

Jon pulled a simple leaflet out from under a stack of papers and read off Hannah's menu. "Mussels and fries with garlic aioli, bacon quiche with arugula, pasta with lemon ricotta, and artisanal grilled cheese sandwich with fresh figs, strawberries, and balsamic glaze." He looked up. "That's what I had. It was excellent."

"Cheese and fresh figs sounds good, but so does the pasta—and the mussels. I need a moment to decide."

"So." Jon set down the menu and wrapped his hands around his water glass. "Have you seen Jenny since the bonfire?"

"No, not since last night," Billie said. "I released my pelican and took care of the cormorant. I also met with the marine biologists at Lizzie May University to find out what our tagged sea lions are doing. It was fun, but it took most of the afternoon."

"Talk about the university." Jon nodded at the door.

Billie looked up. A group of men had come in, talking and laughing and scanning the room for a free table.

"Who are they?" she asked.

"The tall one is Sebastian Ford."

"Ford?"

"He's a history professor at Lizzie May. I don't know the others, but they look like professors too, don't they?"

Billie smiled. The men were wearing blue button-up shirts with rolled-up sleeves and khaki pants. It was the uniform of every male professor she'd ever met.

Sebastian was tall and dark, with blue eyes and a strong jawline that sported the hint of a five o'clock shadow.

Billie sat up with renewed interest. "Isn't he very young for a professor?"

"He's in his early thirties, I believe. He only started recently."

"He just got hired?"

"Two years ago, I think."

Sebastian had spotted them and waved. Jon waved back. Sebastian said something to his friends and then made his way toward them.

"He's awfully good-looking. Do you think it's wrong for a woman to date someone much younger?" Billie managed to say through the side of her mouth before Sebastian reached them.

"The man himself." Sebastian held out his hand. "How are you, Jon?"

"Good!" Jon shook. "This is my sister, Billie."

"Billie. I was hoping we'd meet someday." He offered his hand.

"Enchanted," Billie said and took it. The young professor had a firm shake. She liked it just as much as the strong jawline and the afternoon shadow. "Let me just say that Jon told you only the good bits."

Sebastian laughed and nodded at the empty plate on the table. "Anything on the menu you recommend? I'm hosting a friend. He's interviewing for a tenure-track position in the math department, and I was hoping to wow him with good food into accepting the job."

So the university *was* interviewing for tenure-track positions. Billie turned to Jon. "Don't you have to work? People want their wine."

"Yes, they do." Jon checked his watch and stood. "I should get back and help out." He picked up the food truck's menu and handed it to Sebastian. "All the food is excellent tonight. So is the wine. Just pick whatever sounds best—it won't disappoint. Enjoy." He left.

"Hey." Billie smiled at Sebastian. "Empty tables are sparse tonight. Why don't you all join me? I was just about to order dinner myself."

"That's very kind." He smiled back. "But I'm afraid we'll bore you with our talk about university jobs and the hiring process."

"Not at all," Billie said. "That's exactly what I am interested in. A friend of mine is looking for a job."

"Well, in that case..." Sebastian gestured to his friends, who were still standing, unable to find seating for three. Then he turned back to Billie.

"May I?" He pulled out Jon's stool beside her.

"Absolutely."

He sat. "What's your friend's degree?"

"She has a PhD in history, actually. But she's a bit out of the loop. Can you help her find something?"

Regret crinkled his eyes. "I wish I could! But I can't create positions where there is no funding. Each department has a certain number of tenure lines, and they usually open only when someone leaves."

"You got one," Billie pointed out.

"Only because one of the older professors retired when I happened to be looking for a job. But we don't expect another line to open for a few years at least."

Sebastian's friends arrived, and introductions were made.

The men were called Evan and Miles. Evan looked like a student to Billie and was the one interviewing for a position in the math department. Miles was Billie's age or a little older, a clarinet player, and a professor of jazz music. He took the chair on her other side.

They ordered food from Hannah, and Miles brought wine and water from the bar. When their dinner plates arrived, steaming hot and as large as wagon wheels, Billie asked whether there were other jobs available.

"I applied for a research grant," Sebastian said. "If I get it, I'll need to hire an assistant. Of course, I can't promise I'll get the money, but if I do, I'd be happy to talk with your friend."

"Great," Billie said and felt a fizz of excitement in her belly. Who knew? Maybe this was the windfall Jenny needed. "Can I give you her telephone number?"

"Sure." He pulled a piece of paper and pen from his pocket and slid it over to Billie.

Billie scribbled down both Jenny's and her own number and name.

Sebastian folded the paper and slipped it back into his pocket. "Do you know more about your friend's qualifications?" he asked.

"I'm afraid I don't know much." Billie smiled. "We only just reconnected. She did her thesis on the story of a young whaler who eloped with his sweetheart."

"How romantic," Evan said and pushed his glasses back up.

"It can't have been easy," Billie said reasonably.

"Probably easier than getting tenure. Am I right?" Evan raised an eyebrow at Sebastian as if it was an inside joke.

"For real." Sebastian laughed half-heartedly. "I'd like to chat sometime and learn more about her work."

"She's smart." Billie leaned back. "And she really needs a job. I don't know what she'll do if she can't get one."

"Believe me, I understand." Sebastian set down his quiche as if he had suddenly lost his appetite.

"You all right?" she asked.

"Of course." Sebastian lifted his wine glass and took a long swig.

"Yeah?"

Miles, the jazz musician, reached out and patted Sebastian's shoulder supportively. "It's tough," Miles replied for his friend. "Even if you snag one of the few tenure-track jobs out there, you're on probation for three to five years before you actually get tenure.

There's a committee that will scrutinize your work and make a recommendation to the dean. If you're not living up to their expectations, the dean will kick you back out in the streets. Figuratively speaking."

"Literally speaking, too," Sebastian muttered and drained his glass. "A few years older and less competitive for the job than before."

Billie eyed Sebastian's bacon quiche. It looked and smelled like it tasted *excellent*. Hannah had outdone herself. Billie was lucky not to have had a job so stressful it killed her appetite.

"What do you have to do to prove yourself?" she asked and wondered if consolingly patting Sebastian's hand would be patronizing.

"A lot. Too much. Most of all, I need to publish a paper in a peer-reviewed magazine. I'm cutting it awfully close with the timing. The committee will meet soon."

"How much time do you have?"

"Yesterday is better, if you know what I mean." Sebastian twiddled the stem of his empty wine glass. "I thought I had a solid research project when I applied for the job. But someone in Canada was already working on the same thing. They submitted their study for publication while the ink was drying on my hiring contract. I had to come up with something new. I won't lie—it's been a struggle to find a new project. A lot of false starts. Nothing I do seems to pan out."

"You'll find something." Evan looked miserable on behalf of his friend. "Everyone gets scooped."

"Getting scooped?" Billie asked. "What does that mean?"

"That's when someone does the same research project and publishes before you do." Sebastian turned to Evan. "Getting scooped is one thing. Getting scooped when you don't have tenure is another."

"It'll be all right," Miles said. "Everything will turn out just fine."

"I don't know about that. I really need to find something to research that will get me a quick publication," Sebastian said gloomily. But then he glanced at Billie and rallied a smile.

Billie returned the smile, but she felt bad for having wheedled out Sebastian's worries. He'd come to the winery looking for a good time with his friends, and now he had lost his appetite. "I'm sorry you got scooped," she said quietly.

He nodded appreciation for her compassion. "Well, if I can't come up with a good research project soon, your friend Jenny can have *my* position. At least there is that." The sad joke didn't make anyone laugh.

Billie leaned forward. Bringing up jobs had killed the mood. She wanted to say something to fix her faux pas. "Maybe my friend can help you *keep* your position for yourself. She found an entire armoire full of interesting historical heirlooms in her house. Who knows? Maybe she'll find something of historical significance for you to publish about. Old letters, or a diary, or some interesting object that comes with a story."

Jenny would be happy to help—and helping Sebastian would likely raise her chances of getting hired as his assistant.

"There you go," Miles said and lifted his glass. "That would be good, wouldn't it?"

"That would be something," Sebastian agreed. "Though it's probably more of a fantasy than reality. My specialty is really environmental history, while old heirlooms are more the stuff of social history. Of course, it's possible to change focus." He waved to the bar for another bottle of wine. "It sounds like your friend found herself quite a treasure."

"I know," Billie said. "Though it's not really hers to keep. The hotel belongs to an aunt who never comes around. She's not fond of the Forgotten Cove."

"Hotel? I never heard of a hotel in the cove."

"It's the old Morris mansion."

"*The* Morris? Oscar Morris?"

"The one and only," Billie confirmed. Everyone in the area knew about the historical figure. Even the library was named after him. "Before my friend—her name is Jenny—came back, the hotel stood empty. Back in the sixties and seventies, when her grandmother ran the hotel, it was pretty busy."

"I had no idea."

"It's sort of tucked away in the bushes. But it is mentioned in a book about historic buildings."

Sebastian's face fell. "Oh."

Maybe he'd hoped he could write a publication on the old mansion and felt scooped again? Billie wanted to cheer him up, but she only kept making things worse.

Miles tactfully refilled the glasses. "The dean told me today he's going to cut funding for the jazz choir," he swerved into a new topic. "I had a student crying in my office because of it today. I've been teaching for years and still don't know what to do when the kids start crying."

"Give them tissues?" Billie suggested.

Miles nodded at her; she'd done the right thing to play along. "We need more funding. What's the saying again? We need science to survive, but art is our reason to do so. Something like that."

The conversation turned away from treasure and jobs to the funding crisis of the art department, and Billie was glad for it. She had done her bit to help Jenny.

Clearly, Sebastian was struggling himself and was too junior to have a say in the running of the department. But still, there was a chance he'd get his grant and need an assistant.

If Jenny got the job, she could stay in Mendocino Cove.

Billie's mind drifted from the talk about deans and provosts and things she didn't understand and wasn't interested in.

All of Jon's girlfriends she'd ever met looked like Jenny.

Billie was convinced he had never married because he was holding out for someone more like Jenny.

Maybe, once the two got reacquainted, Jon would decide he had been in love with a memory, not a real person.

Maybe he would decide he still liked her. Then he could ask Jenny on a date.

One way or the other, Jon might finally move forward.

The men laughed, bringing her focus back to the conversation. Miles asked what music she liked. Billie politely replied she liked jazz best of all and decided that tomorrow morning, she would drive over to the hotel and tell Jenny all about Sebastian Ford and his grant.

CHAPTER 26

T he morning fog was like a thick, fluffy marshmallow cloud. Jenny shivered and hooked her arm under Billie's for warmth.

"I'll have to take your word for it that you live in a seaside cottage," Jenny said. "For all I know, I could smack into a redwood tree if I take another step."

"Nonsense. This is a dock, isn't it? There are no docks in the forest. Here, take that. It's nice and warm." Billie extracted her arm and opened a wicker chest, then pulled out two fleece blankets and handed Jenny one.

"Thank you." Jenny shook it out and wrapped it around her shoulders. She should have known better than to leave her sweater at home on a Mendocino Cove morning. But Billie had picked her up for breakfast on the dock, and the truck had been cozy. The blanket was soft and warm, and Jenny's body relaxed.

"The table is at the end of the dock," Billie said and strode forth into the thick fog that swallowed her effortlessly.

"It is?" Jenny squinted. She could see the boards under her feet now. Boards were good. She didn't feel like stepping into the icy Pacific.

"Come on, it's fine. I have breakfast in the fog all the time." Billie laughed. "Hurry up, the coffee is piping hot. It'll warm you up."

"Hot coffee! I'm coming." Jenny took a step. The fog swirled to give her a better glimpse of where she was going. Jenny took another step. "How wide is your dock?"

"Wide. It's basically a pier. I wanted it to be comfortable."

"Okay." Jenny took another step, and another. She could hear the gentle lapping of waves. The fog carried hints of the roses and jasmine Billie had in her garden, and the muted sunlight created a dream-like atmosphere. The wooden boards creaked softly underfoot as she walked on until she spotted Billie's silhouette.

"There you are." Billie waved her closer and sat in one of the two comfortable wicker chairs around a round table that was set with a tablecloth and fine china for a gorgeous breakfast feast.

Jenny pulled off her blanket and sank into the plush cushions of her chair, draping the blanket over her knees. "Oh," she said happily. "This is beautiful."

"You haven't even seen the half of it," Billie replied and poured steaming coffee from a thermos into their mugs. "Just wait until the fog burns up. It'll happen soon. The temperatures are going to be in the 80s today."

"Sounds good." Jenny cuddled deeper into her chair.

"I hope you're hungry."

"I'm starving. What do we get?" Jenny smiled at all the goodies on the table. The smell of freshly baked bread mingling with the floral scent of the fog was delicious.

"First, this." Billie handed her an oversized pottery mug with a pretty red glaze and little white hearts. Then she pointed at a mason jar with a paper straw by Jenny's plate. "That's freshly squeezed orange and grapefruit juice. Let me know if it's too sour."

Jenny first took a sip of hot, aromatic coffee, then of the fresh, tangy juice. "Mmm. It's perfect. And you made heart-shaped waffles, Bills. That's so cute."

"Well, yes. Jon gave me a heart-shaped waffle iron, and there's no point in having another one. They taste the same, whatever their shape."

Jenny bit her lip not to laugh. "I think you just like little hearts. The mug is pretty adorable. Did you make it yourself?"

"Have the waffles with a dollop of cream cheese and honey," Billie said loudly to drown out Jenny and pointed at the breadbasket. "That's Jon's homemade sourdough toast here and Michael's croissants and pastries. He doesn't sell them to just anybody, but I pick some up when I get my newspaper in the mornings." She took the folded-up newspaper that lay beside her chair and showed it to Jenny. "I like the smell of ink and paper. I'm old-fashioned that way."

"I'll read it when you're done." Jenny nabbed a croissant and bit into it. It was still warm from the oven and tasted like a kiss in Paris. "This is so good."

"Have it with butter and this." Billie pushed a small green vase with a bouquet of wildflowers aside so she could reach a glass jar. "Raspberry jam made from wild berries. It's more flavorful than from the store."

Jenny took the small jar and dabbed a spot of bright red jam on her croissant. The fresh flavor exploded in her mouth, followed by the creamy softness of the buttery croissant. "It tastes incredible."

"The raspberries grow behind Jon's vineyard," Billie said and helped herself to a luscious cinnamon roll that was liberally sprinkled with sugar-glazed nuts. "I'm glad we get to have breakfast together after not seeing each other yesterday. I was busy with my birds all day. What did you do?"

"I took down every single curtain in the house and washed it, then started on the hotel linen. The hotel needs a makeover too. The fuzzy Victorian wallpapers really have to go, and some of the upholstery is gloomy too. Almost all the rooms need fresh paint and new pictures and books and plants. If I had the money, I'd redo the place and freshen it up."

"Are the curtains still drying? I imagine it'll take half a second."

"Yes, it will. I hung them up, but I only have so much string and space to drip dry sheets and curtains."

"So, can everyone look inside the living room?" Billie glanced at her.

"If by everyone you mean Polly and the pelicans—yes. They can." Jenny grinned.

"Polly's still hanging around?" Billie looked like she wanted to slap the table.

"She is, but don't worry. I saw her hang out with a bunch of luscious girlfriends, and she flirted with a very nice young man who looks like he makes ten thousand a year." Jenny couldn't help being silly. She was in such a good mood after her night's undisturbed rest.

"Ten thousand? What do you mean?"

"A Jane Austen reference," Jenny explained. "It means you, as Polly's proud mama, are glad he's paying her attention because if they marry, she'll have plenty of pin money."

"You lost me." Billie shook her head. "I'm more of a mystery reader. More coffee?"

"I'm okay, thank you. It's too beautiful of a morning to feel jittery."

As predicted, the fog was starting to lift under the rising sun. Around the dock, water started to glitter and shine like jewels. Mockingbirds called from the lawn, and gulls answered from the sea.

"Guess what." Billie ate the last of her cinnamon roll and wiped her fingers on a napkin.

"What?"

"Yesterday, at the winery, I met someone new. His name is Sebastian Ford, he's gorgeous, and he's up for tenure at Lizzie May's history department."

"Really?" Jenny tore her gaze from the sea. "Are you trying to make me jealous?"

Billie smiled at her over her coffee cup. "On the contrary. I put in a good word for you."

"A good word? What kind of good word?"

"If he gets the grant he applied for, he might need an assistant, and he said he'll get in touch. I gave him both our numbers. I hope that was okay?"

"Of course." It took a second to process what Billie was saying. "He might have a job for me?"

Billie nodded. "What do you think? Did I do good?"

"You did, Billie. Thank you. Working at Lizzie May would be amazing. I hope he gets his grant."

"Can you stay here if you could get a job like that?"

Jenny turned back to the sea. The fog was almost gone. "To tell you the truth," she said slowly, "I don't have anywhere else to go even if I *don't* get the job. My friends in Maine aren't the sort of friends to take me in while I sort myself out."

"Not a single one of them would help out?"

"I don't know. Maybe they would. But I wouldn't be comfortable asking, let alone staying."

"Sheesh, some friends they are," Billie muttered. "You can crash on my sofa as long as you like. I'd even let you have the guestroom." She drained her own heart-covered mug and set it on the table with a firm thud. "How do you feel about organizing another beach bonfire, this time with guests?"

Jenny raised an eyebrow. "Guests like the handsome professor Sebastian Ford?"

"Exactly." Billie began stacking plates and mugs. "We might as well strike while the iron is hot."

"You're right. Let's set up something and send him an invitation." Jenny stood and folded the blankets. They could go back in the wicker chest now. The air had warmed considerably. Either it was that or the excitement of a job prospect at the university.

"The sooner, the better," Billie declared. "I'll text him and see when he's free tonight."

Jenny grabbed the tray and set the breadbasket and jams on it. "I'll go home and finish doing the laundry. The place isn't exactly presentable, with my bedsheets flapping around everywhere."

CHAPTER 27

I brought you this. And also this."

Jenny took the two small wrapped gifts Faye was offering. "You shouldn't have. In fact, I asked you over to pick a few things for the store. I won't be able to catch up dusting the place when every shelf has twenty figurines on it and every wall thirty mirrors and forty framed pictures." The hotel was stuffed to the brim with knickknacks. Jenny wanted to get rid of some of the Victorian clutter and make the place brighter and airier.

"Yes, please, happy to help!" Faye's eyes brightened. "What about Georgie, though? I thought everything belonged to her."

"I emailed to ask if it was okay to clean up the clutter," Jenny said. "And what do you know, she wrote back a line to say sure, get rid of clutter as long as it isn't gold or silver."

"Or jewels," Faye agreed. "Got it. Now open your gifts." She grinned.

"Okay." One package was flat and square, no bigger than her palm. The other was club-like and as long as Jenny's arm from wrist to elbow. "What's the occasion?"

"They're housewarming gifts," Faye explained.

Jenny pulled the delicate tissue paper off the palm-sized square. "How pretty, Faye!" It was a delicate photo frame made of sea glass, holding a photo of Jenny, Faye, Billie, and Ava. "Thank you very much! By the way, do you know where Ava is?"

"She lives in Seattle with her husband, Bruno, and her daughter, Zoe. That's all I know," Faye said. "Billie and I were the only ones to stick around in Mendocino Cove." She smiled. "I made the frame with sea glass we found as kids. I still have a jar full of it if you can believe it."

"You know the story about the chandelier, don't you?" Jenny smiled back. "Grandpa made it from the sea glass collected by generations of women."

"What else are we going to do? We can't throw it back on the beach, can we? Do you like it?"

"I love it. I'll make sure it gets a place of honor, Faye." She set the framed photo on the piano and unwrapped the club-like gift. "Oh. A soup ladle? Thank you very much." She waved the blue wood-and-silicone ladle, scooping air.

"I noticed there isn't one in the kitchen," Faye said, looking satisfied.

"No, there isn't," Jenny confirmed. "Grandma must have tossed it."

"Soup isn't the only thing to ladle," Faye said.

"It certainly isn't," Jenny agreed and put the long handle of the ladle into the back pocket of her jeans to carry around until she went to the kitchen. "Thanks very much for the housewarming gifts. In return, if you see anything you like and it's not silver or gold or jewels, it's all yours."

Faye's eyes flicked to the framed embroidery of the cove and back.

"Sure, take it. You liked it from the moment you saw it." Jenny rounded the grand piano to take the frame off the wall.

"No, Jenny, it's too sentimental. You said you'd never sell it." Faye's cheeks blushed.

"I'm not *selling* it." Jenny took Faye's hand and put the frame in it. "I'm *gifting* it to my best friend who helped take care of my Grandma when I couldn't. It's vastly different."

"Well, then...thanks, Jen. I do love it. I'll hang it up downstairs and won't sell it."

"Good." Jenny studied the wall and chuckled. "Don't come for my wonky X, though. It makes me laugh every time I see it. I haven't laughed much in the last year, so I'm keeping it."

Faye giggled. "Nice try with the reverse psychology. I wouldn't hang that in my house if you paid me. All yours." She put the cove into her drawstring purse and set it on the piano, then clapped her hands. "Right. Hand me some of those rubber gloves and tell me what to do. I only know you finished the laundry."

Jenny handed Faye a pair of housekeeping gloves and pulled on another. "I'd like to get rid of the purple crushed velvet cushions," she said critically. "This room is supposed to be all sunlight and greenery. If I could, I'd redo all the old upholstery and paint the walls and get large, cheerful rugs."

"Rugs are expensive," Faye said. "Especially the large, cheerful ones."

Jenny's thoughts flew back to the gorgeous Ouzaks and Kilims Stan had collected. Some of them had been antique, some new, but they'd all been expensive. Even braided cotton rugs were out of budget right now. "Can you help me with the ladder, Faye? The washed curtains can go back up. At least they're a lot brighter than before."

They pushed the ladder to the window. Faye held it for stability while Jenny climbed as high as she dared and hooked the long, sheer curtain panels back on the rod.

"What a difference," Faye commented as Jenny made her way back down.

"Isn't it?" Jenny jumped to the floor and took a step back. "Hmm." She picked up a tasseled pillow. "These have to go too. No crushed velvet or tassels."

"Let's do it." Faye scooped up an armful of burgundy pillows, brought them to the door, and dropped them into the bins Jenny had put outside. "This is making my eyes itchy." She blinked.

Jenny brought another armful. "Make sure not to touch your eyes. I'll vacuum the upholstery to get rid of some of the dust."

For a couple of hours, they dusted and swept and shifted furniture, pushing sofas and side tables into new places and bringing pillows and extra armchairs into the empty small parlor. The small parlor faced the driveway and had mostly been used to store the guests' luggage, extra beach towels and wicker chairs, and bulky things like baby strollers.

Billie joined them with brand-new mops and self-wringing buckets, and after another stretch of cleaning, Jenny rang the dinner gong and called a break. They sat on the patio and ate pastel-colored macarons and scones with cream.

Jenny drained her iced lemonade and smacked the glass back on the table. "I'm going back in."

Faye wiped lavender crumbs off her mouth. "Let's finish this, baby."

"First I'll finish *this*," Billie declared and scooped extra cream on her scone.

Jenny chuckled and went inside but stopped short by the door. The heirloom armoire had swung open again. She went to it, wiggling the door back and forth. "Why does this keep happening?"

"That armoire was closed a moment ago." Billie came in, still chewing. "The doors need to be rehung. Whatever that means."

"Uh," Faye said from the door where she was brushing sand off her feet. "Are you sure it was closed?"

"Hmm. Yes." Billie poked at the hinges.

Faye joined them. "Have you gone through the things in there yet, Jenny?"

"No, I was too busy with the curtains. The dust was making me itchy."

"To be honest, I'm dying with curiosity about what you'll find."

"Me too." Billie wiped her hands on her old jeans. "Let's look at just one thing before we get back to cleaning."

"You're right. Just one thing," Faye agreed.

"We pretty well went through the things on the top shelf, I think." Jenny moved the boxes they'd already examined to one side. "I should make a list for Georgie."

"What's lying behind the boxes?" Billie pointed. "What's that long thing?"

"I didn't even see that." Jenny stood on tiptoes. "Is it a poster?" She groped for it.

"Is it paper?"

"It is. It's not a poster... It's a scroll." Jenny finagled the scroll out. It had gotten pushed all the way to the back of the shelf, lodging itself in the groove between the shelf and the back.

"It looks old, Jenny," Faye said. "Be careful unrolling it. The paper might be brittle."

"I'll lay it on the piano." Jenny carried the scroll over, her heart beating. She laid down her find. "Billie, hand me another pair of gloves. Not the rubber ones, a pair of medical gloves."

Billie whipped a pair of blue gloves from their carton box and handed them to Jenny. She pulled them on, and slowly, with movements as small and gentle as she could make them, Jenny unrolled the yellowing paper.

All three of them bent over it.

"It's a map," Faye said. "Jenny, this is a really old map."

"Yes, you're right." Jenny traced the squiggly lines and squinted at the few words that were written in an elegant hand. "It's from the nineteenth century." She pointed to the year noted in the middle of the drawing of a compass. "It's beautiful." Her heart was beating a little faster. For a historian, finding old maps was exciting. "It looks like it should be in a museum."

"Where is that?" Billie asked, turning her head to see the map from different angles.

"I think it's here," Faye said suddenly. "Doesn't that look like the cove?"

"You're right." Jenny straightened the paper more in an attempt to decipher the faint words but gave up quickly when the old paper crackled. "Billie, could you take a photo so we can blow it up? I want to let the map curl back up before the paper rips at this fold here. It needs to be restored properly."

"Sure." Billie, who Jenny knew had a good camera on her phone, took several pictures. "Can I send one to Jon? He'll want to see this."

"Of course." Gently, Jenny allowed the paper to curl back into the shape it apparently had held for many years. Then she released a tight breath. "I wonder what the story of this one is. Did Grandma buy it some-where in the area?"

"Maybe it comes from your grandpa's family," Billie suggested. "What do you know about them?"

"Next to nothing, other than they came from here," Jenny admitted.

"Should I send the photo to Sebastian too?" Billie looked up from her phone. "He hasn't replied to the bonfire invitation yet. An old map might be a good way to lure him out of his shell."

"That's a good idea," Faye said. "Maybe he knows someone who can help restore the map."

"Sure, go ahead. I'd like to know what he thinks." Jenny lifted the map gingerly, listening to the crack-ling as the old paper shifted into a tighter roll. She needed to write an email to Auntie Georgie to ask if she would pay for the restoration. "I'm going to put this back where it was. It survived this long. It will last another couple of weeks until I figure out what to do."

Faye fished her phone from her purse and checked the time. "Should we finish cleaning? It's getting late."

They stowed away the map and went to work mopping the floors and polishing the wood until it gleamed. Jenny pushed her hands into her back and straightened with a groan, using her mop as a crutch. "Ugh." She laughed at herself, and then she had a look around. "It looks so much nicer now."

"It's a beautiful room," Faye agreed and pulled her gloves off. The plastic was torn at the fingertips, and she tossed them in one of the white trash bags scattered through the room. "That crown molding is gorgeous."

Jenny squinted at the ceiling and the elaborate decoration. "I have to email my aunt, anyway. Maybe I can talk her into letting me restore the cracks for her."

"It's worth asking."

"Honestly, I don't want her to think about how much money she could make selling it once it's all prettied up." Jenny sighed.

"She wouldn't, would she?"

Jenny only shrugged. She didn't know. "Anything's possible, I'm afraid."

"Hey." Billie had wandered back to the piano where their water bottles stood. "The doors to the heirloom armoire are shut nice and tight. Why *do* they open on their own? Does it happen when you step on a certain floorboard?"

"Maybe it's warped?" Jenny ran a hand over the gap between the doors. "I'll ask Jon to loan me something to smooth out the frame. What's that tool called? A plane. Maybe a plane will do the trick."

Faye let herself fall onto a blue sofa. "As long as it's not opening because it's haunted, you can just tie a rubber band around the handles."

CHAPTER 28

"A plane? Like the tool?" Jon picked a rock off the dry ground around a grapevine and launched it. It flew in a wide, graceful arc through the summer-warm air and plopped into the raspberry bushes. "Why do you need a plane, Jenny?" He smiled at her.

She smiled back. It was too hard not to. Besides, smiles were justified when one was asking for the loan of a tool.

Not justified, however, were deep looks into eyes as blue as the sky over the vineyard.

Jenny blinked and let her gaze wander back to the raspberry bushes whose fruit had yielded Billie's excellent jam. "It's that armoire in the living room," she said. "It keeps popping open on its own."

"And that's bad for morale?" he asked when she didn't elaborate.

She turned back to him, having seen everything there was to see about berry bushes. "Yes, that's right," she confirmed. "It's bad for morale. Mine in particular. It's spooky."

"And the plane will help how?" He picked a lobed grape leaf in passing and handed it to her.

Playing along, Jenny smelled it as if he'd given her a flower. The leaf smelled of warm soil and wood, earthy and solid.

"The vines are early this year." Jon took the leaf from her hand and tucked the long stem behind her ear. "But the flowers are not quite here yet."

"I've never seen grape flowers," Jenny said.

"A grape flower is delicate, pretty, and sweetly fragrant," he said. "And she's always surrounded by others. It's hard to get her on her own."

Her? Jenny blushed warmly and looked away. The breeze that rustled the leaves of the vines tugged her hair over her warm cheeks. When she swept it back, she took the opportunity to let the gifted leaf flutter to the ground inconspicuously.

When Jon invited her to a tour of the vineyard, she knew she shouldn't have accepted. But she did it anyway, just like she'd played along with the leaf-flower. That was her problem.

"So what are you going to do with my plane?" he asked after they'd walked a while and stopped to rub his jaw.

Jenny took a deep breath. "Jon," she said. "I know I'm not doing a good job with"—her finger pointed between them—"I'm sorry."

He looked at her. For a moment, she thought he would say that he had no idea what she was talking about, that she was in for a Victorian moment of having presumed too much. But instead, he nodded. "Neither am I, Jenny. I've become rusty when it comes to matters of the heart."

"I'm not rusty. I've just always been awkward." She smiled and held out a hand. "I had the biggest crush on you when we were kids. Did you know?"

His fingers weaved into hers, warm and strong, and he smiled back.

If Jenny could have stopped time and stayed in the moment forever, maybe she would have done it. But she pulled her hands back and lowered her head to break their shared gaze. "I've had a bad year," she started. "My husband died. And the kids..." She didn't know how to convey that she was grieving while she was laughing, that her kids needed all of her even though they led their own lives and only texted every few days, that she was really traveling when it seemed like she had arrived. How should she say it when she and Jon finally stood here and held hands and talked about love?

Jon wasn't supposed to be her bittersweet love. He wasn't her rebound affair, tinged with sadness and guilt. He was more.

"Hey, it's okay." Jon rubbed a tear off her cheek with his thumb, leaving a burning trail on her skin. "It's okay. We don't have to do anything we don't want. I've waited this long for you. I can wait longer."

She rubbed her own hand over her cheek, more to erase the burn of his skin on hers than to wipe away the tears. "The problem is, I want to do everything. I want *you*, Jon. But I'm a mess, and I can't let you get mixed up in it. You don't deserve that."

He tucked a strand of her hair behind her ear, letting his hand cradle her jaw. "What if I want to be mixed up in your mess? Do I get a vote?"

Jenny blinked the last tear away. "Not yet. But don't go away." She bit her lip. "I didn't mean that. I'm not asking you to wait; I just..." She took a deep breath. "Wait as long as you can, Jon, but no longer. Like I said, I'm still a mess. But I'm trying to sort myself out." She felt herself blush warmly. "I'm not ready for a relationship. I don't want to mess that up too. But I can't stand the thought of you with another woman," she whispered. "I always thought I was a decent person. But I'm not. I'm selfish. When it comes to you, I'm terribly selfish."

He pulled her into his arms. "Me too, Jenny. Believe me, I've tried to go away, and I've tried to stop waiting, and I've tried to forget you. I've tried to do it all. None of it worked. So I'll stick around a little longer and see how you work things out for us." He lifted her chin with a finger. "Listen, don't worry about me. I carry the weight of my decisions. You don't have to do it for me. You don't have to do anything for me other than get back on your feet and let me know when you find out what you want from me."

Jenny rested her forehead on his shoulder and closed her eyes, breathing his scent. "What if I never work it out? What if I'm broken and I can't fix myself? Because sometimes, that's how I feel."

"You're not broken, and you don't need to be fixed," Jon whispered into her hair and pulled her tighter to him. "Nothing can break you. Confusion and grief and not knowing the next right step, those are just the hard bits, the cliffs in the sea. You and me—we are like waves of water crashing into them. We lose our shape as we fly over the rock, and maybe we even spray up in the air and can't remember what we are. But we always rejoin the sea and become whole again."

The corner of her mouth lifted in a small smile. "What does that mean?"

He released her enough so he could look into her eyes. "It means you'll be all right." He smiled back. "Okay?"

"Okay."

"Like water?"

"Like water," Jenny promised.

Slowly, Jon lowered his head and kissed her. It wasn't a peck, and it wasn't passionate or even fully on the lips. It was a brief, tender kiss on the corner of Jenny's smiling mouth.

"Oh," she said softly, wishing for more and knowing she had to say no.

He pulled back, holding her gaze. "Oh is exactly right," he murmured and let her go.

Jenny took a step back and touched her fingers to her lips. "Oh, shoot, Jon," she whispered.

That felt better than she had imagined.

It felt nothing at all like Stan's kisses.

Jon smiled and, with an easy gesture, tucked her under his arm and started walking, so she had to walk with him. Jenny's flustered heart calmed as she walked at his side through sunny row after sunny row of grapevines.

"Look, those are red grapes," he said and pointed at a row of grapevines that looked exactly like the others. "They are the best, but they ripen last. We usually harvest them in the fall, after the green ones. There are some green ones over there." He pointed.

"Fascinating," she said, still tucked under his arm, and put her arm around his waist. It was slimmer than Stan's and the muscles harder. "Red and green, got it. Tell me more."

He ran his free hand through his hair. "The growers over in Napa Valley think they're so cool, with their mild temperatures and perfect soil conditions. Believe me, they're just boys; anyone can grow grapes over there. Don't listen to them. They wouldn't think twice about chatting you up with claims of outrageous mineral contents."

And just like that, he had her laughing again. "Okay," she promised. "I'll be careful." Briefly, he squeezed her to him. "I'm just kidding," he murmured into her hair. "It's not the Napa boys you have to worry about."

"But?"

He growled. "The men of Mendocino County who wring from the dry soil biodynamic Gewürztraminer so sweet it will make you weep."

Jenny laughed and wiggled out from under his arm. "Stop! I mean it." She smiled. "Do you even grow Gewürztraminer?"

He grinned. "No. But I bet I could if I wanted to."

Jon showed her how the vines were tied and pruned and told her where the water for the vineyard came from and what he did to protect early flower buds when there was a frost. When he was done, they had reached the tasting room again.

Faye and Billie's cars were standing in the parking lot. "Is it this late already?" Jon checked his watch. "Yes. It is that late." He pulled open the door for her.

CHAPTER 29

J enny stepped into the cool inside and spotted her
friends. "Hey!" She waved.

"Hey." Faye waved back, smiling broadly.

Billie's eyes traveled between Jenny and Jon,
who'd stopped to push a barrel back where it belonged. "Hey," she said finally, looking disappointed.

Jon went to give her a one-armed hug and shake
Faye's hand. "How are you two?" He nodded at the
glasses filled with white wine. "The new Riesling?
How do you like it?"

"It tastes good," Faye said and drained her glass.
"Almost like juice."

Jon laughed. "Careful. Just because it's young
doesn't mean it's harmless. I think I'd better get you
some snacks."

"Yes, please." Faye refilled her glass and one for
Jenny. "Did you come here on your bike?" She handed her the glass.

"Um, no," Jenny said sheepishly. "I caught a ride."
Jon had picked her up.

"I'm driving all of you back," he called from the room behind the counter. "Especially you and your juice wine, Faye."

Faye giggled and had another sip. "Did you have dinner?"

"Also no," Jenny admitted. "I've been cleaning the upstairs rooms all day. The hotel looks much better now."

"How about lunch?" Billie raised an eyebrow.

"I had a sandwich on the beach. Polly came to talk, and we had a nice little conversation," Jenny reported and tried her wine. The golden drink was vibrant with notes of citrus and floral undertones. "It does taste nice." She took a deeper drink. She was still warm from the sun and Jon's kiss, and now she found she was thirsty. "Mmm. Refreshing."

"Right?" Faye topped up Jenny's glass.

"I'm doing the pouring now," Billie said bossily. "Faye, let go of the bottle."

"Aww, man." Faye lifted her hands as if she'd been the victim of a holdup.

"Calm, calm." Jon was back, sliding a charcuterie tray with an assortment of soft and hard cheeses, meats, olives, crackers, and dried fruits on the table. "Faye, try this; it's yummy."

"Don't mind if I do." Faye stuffed a slice of prosciutto into her mouth, then took another drink and smacked her mouth.

Billie put brie on crackers, topped it with fig jam from a tiny, round glass jar, and handed one each to Jenny and Faye. "My favorite."

Jenny ate it, closing her eyes reflexively as the warm, salty and sweet flavor hit. "It's so good." She took another sip of the cool wine. "Jon, join us." She patted the stool beside her.

"Yeah, join us," Billie said.

The door opened, and a man poked in his head. "Are you open?"

"Almost, but come on in." Jon waved the couple in. Already another car was pulling into the parking lot outside, tires crunching in the gravel. Jon nodded at the women. "I'll have to take a rain check, ladies." He went to the counter and tied a black apron around his waist.

"These aprons look so—" *cute*, Jenny almost said, but she stopped herself at the last moment.

Billie eyed her silently, then looked at Faye, then lifted the bottle. "Another drop, Jen?"

Jenny laughed. "Why do I get the feeling that you're setting me up to talk?"

"Hey, I'm not the one ogling my brother when he brings us cheese or puts on aprons." She grinned and leaned forward. "I'm also not the one who gets custom-tailored vineyard tours."

"Oh, come on, Bills." Faye's words lilted in a sweet singsong. "You get plenny...*plenty* walks. *Walks*."

"Oh, dear. Here, eat a bit more." Jenny made a brie cracker and set it on Faye's plate. "I guess that wine does have a kick."

As if the word inspired Billie, her foot suddenly connected with Jenny's shin.

"Ouch!" More startled than hurt, Jenny looked up.

"There's that jazz musician I told you about." Billie nodded toward the door.

Jenny turned around. Two men, one older, one younger, both wearing button-up shirts in shades of blue and khaki pants, had entered.

Billie stood and waved, and the older man smiled and waved back. "Hi!" Billie said when they arrived at the table. "Nice to see you again!"

"I was just going to say the same." The older man shook her hand, holding it longer than necessary.

" 'S *nice*," Faye said happily, her big eyes going between the two. "You're nice."

"Thank you very much," the man said and offered his hand across the table to Faye. "I'm Miles. And you are—"

"Faye. *Fa*-ye." She shook.

Jenny moved Faye's glass so it wouldn't knock over. "I'm Jenny," she said. "Nice to meet you, Miles."

The younger man turned out to be Evan, the math department hopeful, on his last day of touring town and campus. He dragged two more stools to the table, and the two men joined their little group.

"Where is your friend Sebastian?" Billie asked. She'd been shooting looks at the door, clearly hoping he would still come.

"I don't know. He said he'd meet us for dinner since it's Evan's last day. Let me text him." Miles pulled his phone from his pocket and texted.

An answer dinged back almost immediately.

Miles read it. "He's feeling under the weather; he thinks he cracked a molar biting on an unpopped popcorn kernel. Apparently, it's pretty painful."

"Tell him to go see Dolores Garcia on Main; she'll make time for him if he's in pain." Billie pulled out her phone to look up the number for Sebastian, who texted back that he'd already talked to the dentist's office and was on his way.

They ordered more wine and food once Hannah was set up. Evan talked about his impressions of Mendocino Cove, Lizzie May, and the interviewing process, and Miles told stories from his former life as a jazz musician in San Francisco.

"I'd have liked to meet Sebastian," Jenny told Jon, who was driving her, Faye, and Billie home. The sun had set an hour ago, and the evening sky was blue velvet. "I realize it's unlikely that he'll hire me, but I can't help but cross my fingers, anyway."

Jon hummed something that could've been an agreement or a disagreement or something else entirely. Jenny didn't press the topic. But Billie cleared her throat. "Jenny, Sebastian got scooped. I'm not sure how likely it is that he will get his grant." She told the story of how he had lost his chance at publishing, and how desperate he was to find a new topic to investigate.

Jenny sighed. "It's a problem," she admitted. "Published papers are the currency of the academic world. It's best if he pivots quickly and finds something new to work on."

"The hotel is our first stop since it is closest," Jon said after a while. "Everyone okay with that?"

"I gotta pee," Faye said. She'd stopped drinking shortly when the two professors joined them and recovered a little after sampling the rich charcuterie and cheese board and eating Hannah's honey-glazed chicken and mushroom risotto. "Like, badly."

"I have to pee too," Billie said. "Do you mind if we come in, Jenny?"

"Of course not. In fact, how about a cup of coffee on the beach? You all can say hi to Polly. She's been barking her head off all day for me to come out and play."

"All right," Faye and Billie said at the same time.

"I'd love to, if we make it a short coffee," Jon said. "It's a slow night at the winery, but I don't want Hannah to hold down the fort by herself too long."

"Yeah, and you'd better hope Michael doesn't find out you're poaching her away from him." Billie's voice came from the dark back seat like that of a grim oracle.

"He still doesn't know about the food truck, eh?" Jon grinned in the rearview mirror at his sister.

"Nope. Hannah has a calendar and makes a cross for every day he doesn't ask what she's up to after work. She says it's a scientific study."

"There's Forgotten." Jenny pointed at the hidden turn. "I need to cut back those vines. I bike past myself if I don't pay attention."

"You should call the town to do it. I think they have forgotten the cove too." Jon turned into Forgotten, crossed Beach, then pulled up in front of the hotel.

"Are you going for a juicy electricity bill?" Billie climbed out of the back and jumped onto the ground.

"I must've forgotten to turn the lights off." Jenny frowned at herself. The foyer and storage parlor were brightly lit.

Jon closed the driver's door. "Did you? I don't know why you would have turned the lights on in the first place."

It was true. There'd been plenty of sunlight streaming into the rooms before she left. "I guess it happened," she said slowly.

"Did you lock all the doors?"

"The front door, anyway." Jenny hitched the strap of her purse higher and started walking toward the house. "But I probably left the beach doors unlocked."

Walking beside her, Jon held out a hand to slow her down.

"What?" she asked and stopped to look at him in the dimming evening light.

"Nothing," he said. "But maybe I'll go in first."

"Really?" Her stomach dropped. Had someone broken in?

Jon started walking. "I'll be back in a moment."

CHAPTER 30

F aye squinted at the lights in the window. If only she hadn't had that last glass of wine, maybe the beginnings of a dull ache wouldn't thrum in the base of her head. She shivered and wrapped her arms around herself.

"Jon?" Billie called out into the dark. "Everything okay?" She frowned and turned to Jenny. "How long does it take to look around? I'm going in too."

Behind the house, a sea lion barked.

Jenny checked the glowing screen of her phone. "He's been in there for two minutes."

"Is that long?" Faye asked and massaged her temple.

"It's long if you need help," Billie muttered.

Jenny shot her an alarmed look. "Yeah, let's go in. Two minutes is enough to check the rooms."

"I don't think it is," Faye said reasonably. "Not if he goes to check the upstairs too." Unlike her friends, she felt not a trace of alarm. Just the dull ache at the base of her neck. "I really do have to pee, though."

Without another word, all three started walking toward the house.

"I probably just forgot to turn off the lights," Jenny murmured when she pushed open the door. "Hello? Jon?"

"Yeah. Hi." Jon was jogging down the stairs and met them in the foyer.

"All good?" Billie asked, relief in her voice.

"If you mean is it safe, then yes, I think so. I didn't find anyone hiding under the beds or in the closets. Nothing amiss upstairs at all."

"Oh, good," Jenny said and relaxed her tight stance. "Just a trick of our nerves, then."

"Not quite." Jon waved them to follow. "It looks like you did have an unwanted visitor." He led them through the foyer and into the living room.

Faye entered last, convinced she was going to pee herself any moment. But when she crossed the threshold into the mansion's grand living room, both the urge to pee and the headache disappeared.

"I just cleaned this *up*." Jenny sounded stunned.

Billie stepped aside, and Faye came to a hard stop. "Whoa. What happened here?"

The living room was in disarray. Sofas and coffee tables had been pushed around, flower vases flung to the ground, trinkets carelessly tossed to the floor. The door to the beach was wide open, and a breeze reeking of seaweed and foul tide pools tugged on the curtains.

"Augh. What *is* that?" Faye frowned.

Outside, Polly was barking.

Jenny went to the door and called, "It's all right! Hey—calm down, baby. We're back!"

"Maybe she's upset that a stranger was in here," Billie said distractedly.

"Hey." Lying on the floor, Faye spotted the picture she'd given Jenny as a gift. Several pieces of sea glass had broken off the frame.

"Oh no." Jenny frowned. "I meant to take it upstairs."

"Nothing seems out of place upstairs," Jon said. "It's only the living room that's been ransacked."

"Should we call the police?" Billie had been turning on her heel in a slow circle, holding her phone in the air.

"What are you doing?" Jenny asked.

"I'm taking a video for evidence." Billie stopped the movie and started another one.

"Billie listens to true crime podcasts while she bakes," Faye said. She put her sea glass frame on the piano.

"I'm calling the cops," Billie announced behind them. "Don't touch anything else, you guys. Faye, just leave the sea glass on the ground. Maybe they can find fingerprints."

She dialed and started talking on the phone.

"Is anything missing, Jenny?" Jon asked.

"I can't tell. It's such a mess."

"Check the armoire, Jenny," Faye advised. "Someone was searching for something."

"The doors are open." With a beating heart, Jenny walked to the old closet and rifled through the small boxes, wishing she'd already allowed herself the treat of cataloging the treasure trove. "Hmm. Well, the music box is there, and so is the pocket watch. The ivory cards are here... Wait. Hang on." She lifted on tiptoes and reached into the back of the armoire. Then she fell back on her heels. "For a moment, I thought the map was gone, but it's here as well."

"Are you sure everything's there?"

Jenny looked around. "I just don't know. Billie? Do you spot anything? Remember seeing anything when you were cleaning that's now missing?" Her voice rose nervously.

"No, I'm sorry, I don't know what all was in the room," Billie said. "The cops are on their way. Dispatch said two minutes."

Faye crossed her arms. "Where's the silver?"

"It's here. Should I touch it to look inside, Billie?" Jenny was still busy scanning the armoire.

"Better let Gabriel have a look first," Jon replied.

"Gabriel?" Jenny looked at him.

"An old friend who recently moved back to Mendocino Cove," Jon explained. "We went to school together. He was a homicide detective in San Francisco but decided to transfer back home to take care of his dad."

"Oh." Faye's eyes widened. "Why are you bringing up homicide detectives, Jon?"

"I'm just saying Gabe is one of the best," Jon said. "There's only a small handful of cops in the local PD, so everyone works everything as needed. It's just good to know he's the one coming over."

"That's him," Billie said and nodded at the blue and red lights swirling in the foyer.

"I'll let him in," Jon said.

A moment later, he returned with a tall, plain-clothed man in the door.

"Hi, everyone," Gabriel said. He sounded tired, but the sharp blue eyes scanning the room and the people standing in it were wide awake. "I'm Detective Gabe Blackwell."

"Hi," they all said back.

That was quite the name. Blackwell. Gabriel Blackwell. Faye liked it.

Blackwell pulled out a notebook and flipped it open. "Billie said you came home and found the patio door open and the room ransacked."

Faye nodded.

His blue eyes landed on her like a raptor on a rabbit. She could almost feel the talons hooking into her. "Yes? No?"

"Yes," Faye said quickly. "Yes, that's right."

"What's your name, Miss?"

Miss? Why not ma'am? "Uh. Faye."

He stared at her for a beat. "What's your *last* name?"

"Oh. Um—"

He raised an eyebrow, his pencil poised.

"It's Faye McAllister," Billie said and gave Faye a *what's wrong with you* shake of the head.

"Faye McAllister." Blackwell turned back to her, and the raptor landed again. "That's quite the name, Miss McAllister."

"Takes one to know one, Mr. Blackwell."

Was that supposed to be a smile, the crooked way his mouth lifted in the corner?

"Uh, *detective*, what should we do?" Jenny asked, also shaking her head at Faye.

Faye frowned. She hadn't done anything. She didn't even feel tipsy anymore.

Blackwell flipped his notebook shut again. Faye narrowed her eyes. What about the names of the others? He hadn't written *them* down.

"Talk to me," he said, as if he were good company. "Is anything missing? Do you know who might have had a reason to do this?"

"It looks like nothing is missing. But we haven't really looked yet." Jenny turned to the armoire. "This is my grandmother's collection of valuable artifacts. But I don't know everything that was in here."

"Ma'am, don't touch anything, please. Did you all touch stuff?" Blackwell said grumpily.

"I went around the house to make sure nobody was hiding," Jon said. "And we all walked around the living room."

"I *told* them not to touch anything," Billie said importantly. "Because fingerprints and evidence."

"Well, you were right, Billie." Blackwell's voice was suddenly less raptor and more teddy bear. "It would make my life a lot easier if people would stop *touching* things." His eyes landed back on Faye.

"What? Why me?" she asked. "*I* haven't touched anything."

"What's that?" He pointed at the piano.

"That's a piano," she said.

His face turned even more into a deadpan mask. "What's that on it, Miss McAllister?"

"She picked up the photo frame." Billie grinned, obviously delighted to rat Faye out.

"Uh-huh." Blackwell nodded. "Well, well."

For a moment, Faye thought Blackwell would pull out the notebook again, but instead, he moved to open the door he'd been blocking. "I need you to leave the house, please. Just wait out front for me. You live here?" He looked at Jenny.

"I do."

"Can you stay the night somewhere else?"

"I can stay with Billie."

"Do you need anything, a toothbrush, PJs, medications, that sort of thing?"

"I have a toothbrush and PJs for you, Jen," Billie said.

"That's all I need. And this." Jenny picked up her purse.

Blackwell nodded. "I'll be out with you in a minute."

They made their way through the door, careful now not to step on anything that might be evidence.

"Are you sure nothing's missing?" Blackwell asked casually when Faye passed him.

He made it sound like she was missing a marble, or maybe, a heart.

"We *don't know*," she said icily and swanned past him into the night.

CHAPTER 31

Three days after the break-in, Jenny was sitting down for breakfast on Billie's breakfast dock. Billie poured coffee, and Faye was sleepily scooping sugar into hers.

Jenny put a spoonful of brown sugar in her mug and topped it with a dollop of cream and a pinch of cinnamon cocoa. It was already warm and sunny and bright, and while the view was beautiful, she almost missed the mysterious morning fog and the cozy blankets. She smiled at how spoiled she'd become and sat up to survey the feast on the table.

"How crazy early did you get up to make all this, Billie?" Faye helped herself to a stack of fluffy pancakes with blueberry syrup, breakfast sausages, and a colorful jar of overnight oats with layers of raspberries, walnuts, and chocolate.

"The cormorant gets up with the sun," Billie said. "Maybe slightly before." She ladled eggs Benedict on plates and slathered them in creamy hollandaise sauce.

"You should always have a hungry cormorant." Jenny smiled and poured her friend a glass of the freshly squeezed orange juice. "How is she doing, by the way?"

She sat back down and bit into her strawberry and cream croissant.

"She is gaining weight quickly," Billie said. "I think she just had a string of bad luck hunting."

"I wish we had a bakery in town. It would be nice not to have to drive so far for fresh bagels and breads," Faye said vaguely.

"How about it, Jenny?" Billie asked through a mouthful of lemon waffles. "Do you want to open a bakery?"

"I would if I had the starting capital." Pensively, Jenny looked out at the Pacific Ocean. "And if I weren't so hopeless at, you know, *baking.*"

"You can't bake?" Billie asked, sounding surprised.

"Not a bit," Jenny admitted. "Baker's yeast is a mystery to me. So is the difference between baking powder and baking soda. Why are there two? Why can't one be enough?"

"Ah," Billie said. "Then I think I agree. You're better off doing something else."

Jenny nodded wisely.

"Have you heard from Gabe?" Billie looked up.

"We talked. He said they didn't find any fingerprints other than our own. Guess what they *did* find?"

"What?"

"Seaweed."

"Oh." Faye had frozen at the mention of Gabe, but now her eyes widened. "Like my ghost!"

Billie shook her head. "It's only a ghost when you *can't* find it, Faye. Once you do, it's just another bit of seaweed."

"What if the ghost of a drowned sailor dragged it in? How about that?"

Billie groaned. "Yeah right, Faye. Sheesh."

Jenny chuckled.

"What's funny?" Faye asked. "Aren't you worried that some precious artifact you didn't even know about was stolen?"

"Gabe and I discussed it. We think we know who broke in."

"Who?" Billie and Faye looked up together.

"Polly. I think Polly missed me and came to have a look." Jenny smiled. "Gabe agrees."

"Polly?" Billie looked aghast. "She would never. Would she?"

"She was pretty darn close to the house when I told her not to bark."

"It did smell like her too," Faye said. "Now it makes sense."

"That's why everything was tossed around willy-nilly. Polly was probably bumping into things trying to find the door again."

"But you don't know that." Billie popped the last bite of waffle in her mouth.

"You can take a whiff of the sofas yourself." Jenny shivered. "Everything smells of sea lion. I'll need to get a rug cleaner with an attachment for upholstery. And a cleaning solution with a lot of citrus in it."

"What are we going to do with Polly?" Billie asked. "What if she cuts herself on Faye's sea glass frame next time?"

With an offended look, Faye grabbed the newspaper that lay folded on the table and shook it open. "Polly sits on sea glass all day long. And broken shells. And pointy sticks."

"I'll make sure to close the door from now on when I'm gone," Jenny promised. "Gabe and I met for coffee, and he properly told me off for not locking up. I guess it is safer than relying on people missing the turn onto Forgotten."

"Especially now that you have a whole treasure trove in the house," Faye said from behind her newspaper. She sounded more awake and cheerful after her second coffee. "This is the life, isn't it? Eggs Benedict, the glittering ocean, the—" She broke off abruptly and lowered the paper. "Wait, you met with Blackwell for coffee?"

"Yes. He invited me."

"What?" Faye frowned. "That's incredibly unprofessional of him. Billie, they can't do that, can they?"

"Do what? Have coffee? I believe they're allowed to have coffee. Um." She cleared her throat. "Was Jon with you?"

Jenny smiled. When would Billie just come out and ask? "No, he wasn't. Why would he have been?"

"No reason."

"Okay."

"Did you only talk about the house or about private stuff too?" Faye demanded.

"Both. He's very nice." Jenny swallowed a laugh at how annoyed Faye was. In fact, her feeling had been that Gabe mostly wanted to know more about Faye. He'd seen Faye around town but never made her acquaintance.

"I don't care. That's *so* unprofessional." Faye lifted her paper back up and hid behind it.

"Has Sebastian called you?" Billie asked. "I was hoping he would get in touch. Regardless of his grant. Or, I suppose, his toothache."

"I'm sure he has other things to do."

"Hopefully, he's working hard on establishing a new research project."

"Listen," Jenny said and leaned back. "I should offer Sebastian the map."

"You should?" Billie looked up.

"It sounds like he badly needs a new project, and I believe the map is historically significant. Even just finding out who made it could get him the publication he needs."

"Oh my goodness!" Faye said. "You could do that—or you could even do the research yourself! It's a way to get back into business!"

"What?" Billie leaned forward as well.

"Look." Faye folded the newspaper and laid it back on the table. "Jenny is just as desperate for a job as Sebastian. And, no offense, but she's older and out of the loop. It's harder for her in the job market. If you have a way back into the game, why not take advantage of it?"

"That's true," Billie said. "You are under no obligation to help Sebastian. Don't you agree?"

Jenny nodded. The thought had occurred to her. But without a university affiliation, it was unlikely she would get a research paper accepted for publication. No acquisitions editor worth her salt was interested in the musings of a private person, whether or not they had a degree. Besides... She sighed. "Maybe it's my trauma from my husband's death, maybe it's because Sebastian was willing to help me, maybe it's because he's of similar age as my son. I don't know. But I want to help him."

"I understand," Billie said.

"Have a pancake, Jenny," Faye said soothingly, putting one on Jenny's plate and spooning whipped cream and blueberry compote over it with motherly concern.

Jenny smiled at Faye's fussing and picked up her fork. "It's good to have you two for friends," she said. "I'm so grateful we reconnected, and I love you to bits."

Billie looked out at the ocean and cleared her throat. "Well..."

"What?" Faye served Billie a pancake too and pushed the fork and the compote closer, all but patting Billie's head. *Now you made her cry*, she mouthed at Jenny.

"Stoppit, Faye, I'm *not* crying." Billie picked up the fork and ate some cream and berries. "Jenny, maybe you and Sebastian can work on the map together."

Jenny helped herself to another pancake. They were fluffier than normal ones, puffed up to almost twice the size.

"That would be great," she admitted. "In fact, I couldn't do it by myself. I need access to a university library and professional journals and peers, and who knows what machinery to test for age and originality. I can't just wander into the local branch of the public library and hope to find relevant sources."

"Well then, working together is the solution!"

"Only if the stars align." Jenny finished the second pancake. "Maybe he's not interested. Maybe there is not enough material for a paper. Or he might not want a second author on his publication."

"That seems rather selfish," Billie said and refilled their coffee mugs. "Why should that be?"

"It depends on his tenure requirements," Jenny said. "A single author doesn't have to share the laurels."

"Let's see what he says."

"The faster, the better, since his committee will meet soon. Let's not even set up an appointment. Let's just go right now and stop by his office."

Billie stood. "I'm coming with you," she announced. "I'll make sure he plays nice."

Faye rose as well, stretching her arms. "I'm coming too. I just want to know what happens next."

CHAPTER 32

They piled into Billie's truck and drove straight to the Lizzie May campus in Maytown. The university stood on a low bluff that overlooked the ocean. Billie found a spot in the student parking lot, and they jumped out.

"Let's see." Billie put on her sunglasses. She had been to the university plenty of times to talk with marine biologists and specialty vets about her rescue charges and liked coming here. "The history department is in that big old building over there."

"That one?" Jenny eyed the brick building with tall windows Billie was pointing out. "What a view they have!"

They started walking. "It's a gorgeous campus," Billie confirmed. "I came here to study biology and loved every moment."

The closer they got, the more students milled about. They carried backpacks and books and lunches from the cafeteria, laughing and chatting with each other or scrolling on their phones.

"I guess the semester is almost over," Faye said.

A girl wearing lemon-yellow headphones bumped into her. "Sorry! Sorry," the girl mumbled and hurried on, still looking at her phone.

"Never mind," Faye called after her. "Goodness, so busy," she said, turning back to Billie and Jenny.

"It's final exams," Jenny said. "My daughter Audrey has hers too. It's stressful."

"Is Audrey a good student?" Billie asked to give Jenny a chance to talk about her daughter.

"Yes, she is." Jenny nodded. "I was worried she'd struggle when her dad died, but her professors made sure she got through the semester. She picked up right where she left off."

"You must be proud of her," Billie said and started walking again. The last time she talked with her sons, Ben and Louis, was almost three weeks ago. It was time for a visit.

"In here," she said and pulled open the heavy door to the building that housed the school of humanities. "Let's see."

She browsed the tall brass directory that hung on the wall.

"Room three oh six," Faye said and pointed. "Dr. Sebastian Ford."

Billie nodded. "Right." She waved to the others to follow her. "I know where that is."

A few minutes later, they arrived in a long corridor with doors left and right, some open, some closed. Sebastian's was open, and they gathered in front of it. He was sitting behind a desk that was facing the door and looked up when they blocked the light from the corridor.

"How very ominous." He smiled, put down his pen, and stood to greet them.

"Are you busy?" Billie asked.

"I'm grading exams." Sebastian gave a fleeting smile. "It's nice to see you, Billie. Please come in. And uh, close the door a little, if you don't mind. Otherwise, students will wander in every other second. They're wild to argue for better grades right now, as if they didn't have all semester to work on them."

"Sure." Billie let the others file into the office before her and closed the door without latching it. "Sebastian, this is my friend Faye, and this is Jenny, whom I told you about."

"Nice to meet you," Jenny said. "I hope you don't mind us barging in like this."

"Of course not. I do have a class in fifteen minutes, though. Another exam." He gave the clock on the wall a harried look.

"We can come back later," Faye said.

"No, no, you're here right now. Frankly, there never is much time. Please, sit." Sebastian pointed at the chairs grouped by a bookshelf full of textbooks. They scooted them to the desk and sat, and he took his chair and folded his hands. "What can I do for you?"

"Well," Jenny said and smiled. "I just moved back into my grandmother's old house."

"Yes," Sebastian said. "Billie mentioned it. The historic home, right? Do you have a question about the original owner or the architecture?"

"Many, but that's not why I'm here. I found an old map my grandmother owned. I think you might be interested in it."

"I texted you a photo," Billie said suddenly. She had gotten back a reply from her brother, but not the professor. "Did you look at it? You never replied."

"A photo? No, I don't think I..." He tapped on his screen. "Yes. Here it is. I'm sorry, I'm not very good at keeping up with my emails and texts. It's the students. They're forever writing for no good reason, and if I reply, they reply, and on and on it goes. Usually downhill."

He zoomed the picture out. "Whoa," he said. "That looks genuine."

"I think it is. I think it is an early map of the coast of Mendocino Cove," Jenny said. "See this?" she pointed. "That must be Mendocino Island, don't you think?"

"And you say your grandmother owned it?"

"Yes."

He looked up. "Don't tell me it's my lucky day and you want to sell the map?"

"It's not mine to sell," Jenny said. "It's my aunt's. But I want you to use it for your research if you're interested in it. It could have historical significance if you find out who made it and why."

"You want me to look into it?"

Jenny nodded. "Yes. I hear you need a quick publication to meet your tenure requirements. Maybe this could be it."

Sebastian put his hands back down on the desk, spreading them wide. "Listen." He smiled, but his eyes were wary. "I know Billie told you I applied for grant money to pay an assistant. But I might never get it. Even if I do, I'll have to hire whoever is best qualified for the job. Are you aware of that?"

"Yes," Jenny said. "Of course I am. Would you like to stop over tonight to have a look at the map? You can always say no if you're not interested."

"I would," Sebastian said. "I can't say I know much about maps, but my last project fizzled out. I couldn't get it off the ground, so I need a new research project."

"Good."

Billie leaned back. It wasn't the enthusiasm she'd hoped for, but maybe enthusiasm was too much to expect when maps weren't his area of expertise. For a fleeting second, she hoped he wouldn't accidentally damage the fragile map, not knowing what he was doing.

A gentle knock, and the door behind them opened fully. "Dr. Ford?"

Sebastian stood. "Dr. Perez. Come in."

Billy turned.

A small, wiry woman wearing hiking boots stood there, her eyes locked with Sebastian's. "Good morning, everyone," Dr. Perez said pleasantly and brushed her silver-streaked hair back. "I'm Carolina Perez, the head of the history department. I came to ask Dr. Ford for a meeting. I hope I didn't interrupt anything important?"

"Oh." Jenny stood. "We were just about to leave."

"I think it's time for a conversation, Dr. Ford," Dr. Perez said. "Lana will start off your students with the mandatory class evaluations, so we still have a few minutes. Could you see me in my office?"

Billie turned back to him, ready to get up and leave.

She saw Sebastian nod. But what struck her was the way the color drained from his face. It reminded her of the way the tide drains from a tidal flat. Fast, and seemingly forever.

"Of course, Dr. Perez," Sebastian said. "Ladies... I'll see you soon."

They all stood to leave.

Billie bit her lip as the young professor passed her. Had Jenny's offer of the map been too late? He looked miserable.

"Feel free to share what I said about the map with Dr. Perez," she heard Jenny whisper to Sebastian.

Dr. Perez looked back over her shoulder. "Oh, and Dr. Ford... Bring your coffee. We'll take our time."

CHAPTER 33

J enny raked her fingers through her wind-swept hair and glanced in the large oval mirror that hung in the foyer. After cleaning up Polly's mess, Jenny had spent the day out on the rocks, watching the waves crash against the rugged, wild shore for hours. The salty breeze had left her hair in tangles, but she didn't care.

Being out there, with only the sound of the sea and her thoughts, was healing. Each crashing wave chipped a piece off her grief and washed it into the sea. The sea, that great mother and grave, wrapped it in sea-foam and carried it out to the middle of the world, where it sank to the bottom and disappeared forever.

Now, Jenny opened the door. The sun was setting, casting a warm orange glow over the world.

Sebastian had called her after their talk in his office in the morning. He thanked Jenny for trying to help, but he wasn't going to pursue the matter of the map. Tenure was out of the question. After overhearing their discussion while talking to a student in the corridor, Dr. Perez had gently but clearly spelled it out for Sebastian.

Jenny offered to meet and talk things over, but the young man wanted some time on his own.

"I need to do some soul-searching," he said. "I need to figure out what's next. Thank you for trying to save me. But I think we each have to save ourselves. There's no other way."

Soon after that, Dr. Perez had called Jenny and asked if they could meet.

Now the head of the history department stood outside the hotel, holding a huge bouquet in her hands. When she saw Jenny, she held it out. "Hi," she said. "I've brought you flowers."

"Goodness. Thank you." The flowers filled Jenny's arms. They smelled sweet and fresh, and she couldn't help but smile at the unexpected gift. "You didn't have to do that."

"Yes, I did." The graying strands in Dr. Perez's hair glittered like burned gold in the evening light.

Jenny stepped aside. "Please, come in."

"Thank you." Dr. Perez entered, and Jenny closed the door. "What a peculiar chandelier. I've never seen one quite like this."

"My grandfather made it for my grandmother. You could say it was a labor of love." Jenny smiled fondly at the blue and green dots dancing across the room. "Come this way. I thought we could sit outside and enjoy the sunset."

"Sure." Dr. Perez followed her through the corridor with its wallpapers and glass display cases and framed paintings, past the grand piano and the comfortable couches, curiously looking around. "You have a beautiful house. I had no idea it was here until Sebastian told me about it. He said it belonged to Oscar Morris?"

"Morris built it for his mother, but she didn't want it. I think he tried so hard to forget about the expensive failure that it affected the entire cove." Jenny smiled. "Let me put these in a vase."

"I got a mix of roses, lilies, and daisies. Bright colors to say thank you on behalf of the department." Dr. Perez adjusted her glasses. "What you did was very kind. Not everyone would make such a generous offer."

"I'm just sorry it didn't help him in the end." Jenny shook her head.

"Research wasn't the only concern his committee had. He told me himself that he didn't enjoy working with students as much as he'd thought he would. Of course the students picked up on it and returned the sentiment. Getting locked into tenure would not make Sebastian happy. I think he would be happier in another job, and the sooner he re-orients himself, the happier he'll be."

From everything Jenny had seen, Dr. Perez was correct. Jenny had known plenty of professors. Most enjoyed their students and suffered from too many ideas for research projects, not too few. In comparison, Sebastian just seemed miserable.

"Are you all right?" Dr. Perez adjusted her glasses.

"I never should have offered him the map. I should have known better."

"Not at all. You did your best to help one of our faculty, and the entire department appreciates your kindness. It's good to know there are people like you and your friends."

Jenny nodded. "Is Sebastian still at the university?"

"He'll wrap up his work with the semester. Exams end today, so he's pretty much free to leave as soon as he has posted the grades. The rest can be finished online."

"I'm worried about him."

"Don't be. He will recover from this blow." Dr. Perez's smile was reassuring. "I've been the head of the department for a long time. Tenure requirements at Lizzie's are tough. Even our pre-tenured professors are incredibly smart, capable people. Sebastian just hasn't tapped into his passion yet."

"I hope he finds it," Jenny said and rose. "Make yourself comfortable, Dr. Perez," she said. "I'll only be a second." Jenny's arms were growing moist with water from the stems of her flowers. Grandma's large crystal vase was perfect for the bouquet.

"Can I help?" Dr. Perez opened and closed her hands.

"I'm just going to put the flowers in water before they wilt."

"All right. Thanks, Mrs. Summers."

"Jenny, if you don't mind."

"Thanks, Jenny." For the first time since Jenny had met her, Dr. Perez smiled. The skin beside her eyes crinkled into a pattern that was as well worn as her frown lines. "I'm Carolina."

"I'm glad you stopped by, Carolina." Jenny smiled back. She went to get the vase and arranged the bouquet on the teak table.

Carolina took one of the wide wicker chairs, and Jenny joined her after adjusting the patio umbrella so they had shade. She shamelessly filled her plate with the goodies she'd put out earlier.

"Listen," she said when Carolina took a single mini empanada. "A quick bite won't do. You have to try everything." She picked up a seared scallop with soy-ginger glaze and set it on her plate. "These are very good, for example."

"I had one of the mini empanadas before you came," Carolina admitted. "Where did you get them? You didn't make them yourself, didn't you? Please tell me that I can buy them in a store."

"I can't cook two pennies worth," Jenny said cheerfully. "But they're not from the store, either. I'm lucky to have friends who cook, and they brought me the platter this morning. It's way more than I can eat by myself. I'm glad you came over." She poured generous glasses of cool white wine, wiping the condensation off Grandma's hotel crystal with a paper napkin.

The professor leaned forward, interested. "What's this?"

Jenny pointed. "Prosciutto-wrapped asparagus spears, pesto and goat cheese bruschetta, mini quiches with bacon, cheddar and chives." She pulled the second plate closer. "Fresh fruits and a honey-yogurt dip, lemon curd and raspberry tarts, chocolate strawberries and cream puffs, coconut macaroons with dark chocolate ganache."

"Your friends made all of these?" Carolina's eyebrows rose. "You have nice friends. I'm a little jealous."

"Frankly, I don't know about the cream puffs," Jenny said. "They do seem very much like the ones I saw at the market."

Carolina ate a lemon tart. "Did you come here after a divorce?" She nodded at Jenny's hand. "I see a wedding band tan line."

"Oh. No." Instinctively, Jenny tucked her hand out of sight. But then she took a deep breath. "My husband passed away. I only took my wedding ring off a couple of months ago."

"I'm so sorry," Carolina said. "I didn't mean to bring up painful memories. I was so sure you were in love."

Jenny felt a warm blush on her neck. "What about you?"

The laugh lines crinkled deeper. "I'm divorced. But unlike you, I'm not a particularly nice person, so I don't expect to fall in love again."

They tried the cool golden wine and ate the scallops and strawberries while they talked about historical houses.

"That was delicious," Carolina said eventually and folded her napkin. "But I didn't come here to eat. I came to talk about your conversation with Sebastian."

"Yes?" Jenny tilted her head. "What about it?"

CHAPTER 34

S ebastian showed me the photo of your map. I would love to know more about it." Carolina cleared her throat. "But if it was meant for Sebastian's eyes only, that's okay."

"You are welcome to it."

Carolina smiled. "Thank you. I was hoping you'd say that."

"It's not entirely selfless," Jenny said. "I'm dying to find out more myself, but I'm not in a position to do much research."

"I understand you have a degree in history. Sebastian pulled up a few of your papers to look at what you do, and I had a glimpse. I like your work. Very meticulous and with broad public appeal. That never hurts when applying for funding."

They had looked at her publications? "Thank you." Jenny took a breath, deciding to charge ahead. "If you ever need an assistant, let me know."

"That's the other reason I came." Carolina smiled. "Sebastian's grant won't get funded since he got scooped. But now that he is leaving, we'll need a stand-in to teach his classes until we can organize a new search. They're introductory classes. You probably taught them as a grad student."

Jenny nodded and took another sip of her wine to stay calm.

"It's only an adjunct salary, but it'll get you by in Mendocino Cove. More importantly, it's a foot in the door for better jobs. Would you like to do it?"

"Yes, I want to do it," Jenny said weakly. "Absolutely."

The professor leaned forward, her dark eyes holding Jenny's. "If you're willing to put in a little extra work and maybe even co-publish a paper with me...well. Once the new search comes out, I think you'll have a real chance."

"What do you mean?" Jenny couldn't believe what she was hearing. Did she really have a chance at getting a tenured position?

"This is what I mean." Carolina smiled. "You ease into teaching this coming summer semester. In the fall, you apply to be Sebastian's one-year replacement and start doing research with me to get your publication record back on track. The following fall, we'll run the new tenure-track search, and you apply for the real deal."

"Whoa."

"Are you interested?"

"I'm *stunned*. Yes. Yes, I'm very much interested. I never thought... I never thought I'd get a second chance doing a job I love."

"Lizzie May likes to hire local. You'd be a great fit for our department."

"I feel like I've just won the lottery."

"I like your research, and your generous offer and your kind attempt to help one of the junior faculty warms the cockles of my cold, old heart."

"I don't think your heart can be very old or cold," Jenny said.

"You'll see. I'm not always on my best behavior."

"So...what do I do next?" Jenny tilted her head, half waiting for a catch still to come.

"For now, come see me at the university next Monday," Carolina said. "I'll ask human resources to get the paperwork ready to hire you for the summer semester. Brush up on your teaching skills. Once we start looking for a replacement for Sebastian, and you decide to apply, you'll want to give a guest lecture that blows the dean off his feet." She set down her empty wine glass. "I'll tell you a secret if you promise not to share."

"Oh, secrets." Jenny leaned forward. "What is it?"

"I don't really drink wine so often," Carolina whispered. "But I didn't want to say no." She hiccuped, and her hand flew to her mouth. "Oops."

"Well, there's very little left in the bottle now," Jenny whispered back and doled it out between them.

Carolina picked up her glass. She squinted at the golden wine sloshing in it, then straightened to her not very considerable height. "You know what, I have a very low tolerance for wine. It is delicious, but I had better not drink it." She set down the glass again and primly folded her fingers. "Oh heck," she said a second later and picked the glass up again. "It's a bit of a special occasion, isn't it?"

"Have a tart with a dollop of cream," Jenny advised and pushed the dessert plate closer. "The lemon curd will soak the alcohol up."

Carolina nibbled a lemon tart while she gazed out at the ocean. "What a loud sea lion," she remarked.

Jenny popped open a silver thermos carafe and poured them both coffee. "That's Polly," she said. "She doesn't like to be ignored, but she'll calm down if you wave at her."

Carolina waved. Polly barked a last hello and threw herself happily into the waves to rejoin her other family.

"Ha. How about that?" Carolina emptied her wine.

"Sugar?" Jenny nodded at Carolina's steaming cup.

"Oh. No, black as the night and bitter as lost love, please."

Jenny bit back a smile. "Same." For a sunny half hour, they drank strong coffee and sampled sweet treats and talked about the history department.

"I was wondering." Carolina put down her empty cup. Her gaze had regained focus. "Might I have a tour of your house? It must be one of the oldest in the county."

"Sure." Jenny wiped her hands on her napkin. "Would you like to do it now?"

"I would love to."

They went inside. Immediately, Jenny's gaze fell on the open armoire. "I really need to fix these doors." Jenny wiggled one of the wooden offenders back and forth, trying to figure out why they kept moving on their own. She'd already smoothed out the frame and tightened the hinges. But maybe they needed to be looser?

"Good golly. What's this?" Carolina reached past Jenny. From under a stack of the hotel's best table linens, she pulled out something large, solid, and yellowish-white.

"Oh, what? Wow." Jenny had finally gone through the contents of all the little boxes and loose treasures on the top shelves, but she hadn't gotten to unfolding the bumpy tablecloths and quilts in the lower shelves. Now, she blinked at the tapered object.

Almost as long as the distance from her wrist to her elbow, she recognized the object to be the tooth of a sperm whale. As if that wasn't extraordinary enough, long, thin lines crisscrossed the surface. They weren't random—someone had carved the intricate designs.

"It's scrimshaw art!" she exclaimed.

"It is. Engravings done in bone." Carolina inspected the tooth. "What beautiful scrollwork. Sailors used to make these to pass the time on a long journey."

She handed the tooth to Jenny, who turned it in her hands to follow the lines of the carvings. The entire surface was covered with details. At first glance, she spotted whales, a ship, palm trees, an oval face with almond eyes.

"I came across a few of these when I worked in Nantucket." Jenny reverently set the tooth on the grand piano. "There's a story in the carvings. The trick is to decipher what it is."

Carolina glanced at her. "We don't have anyone in the faculty working on this after the last retirement, but it's up your alley, isn't it? The students are forever asking about classes in maritime history. They want pirates, they want treasures and whales." She licked her lips as if she were a hunting cat. "Did you teach that sort of thing?"

"My professor did. I was his teaching assistant for five years. The classes always had long waiting lists." Unlike Sebastian, Jenny had enjoyed engaging her students with the ocean and its secrets, the joys and sorrows of the people who had wrestled with waves and whales for a living.

Carolina looked at her with interest. "Perfect! We need to talk about developing a new class right away. The students will be happy."

Jenny's head was starting to swim. "I didn't mean to profit off of Sebastian's misfortune," she said weakly.

The professor waved her hand. "Misfortune fiddle-sticks, my dear. He didn't stumble over a stick. Do you think he would need help if he really wanted to be a professor? No." She energetically straightened the stack of tablecloths that had covered the scrimshaw tooth.

"No," Jenny admitted. "I don't think that anymore."

"Just a word of advice. Don't leave the tooth lying around. You can bring it to the university, if you want to store it safely."

"Thank you." Jenny wanted to have a look first, but the armoire wasn't the best place for her grandmother's treasures. "Would you like to see the rest of the house now?"

"Yes, I would. Was this wall added later?" Carolina pointed and walked off, and Jenny followed, explaining what little she knew about the house.

Why did Grandma have all these precious things?

Where did they come from?

CHAPTER 35

Y ou *enjoy* teaching? I'm terrified of speaking in front of a crowd. My heart starts to race, and my hands get clammy." Billie levered open the container of paint and stirred, then dipped her paintbrush. "Uh. This isn't pure white, Jenny."

"Pure white seemed too hard with all the sunlight in here. This has just a touch of yellow in it. It's called sugar lemon."

Billie groaned. "Sugar lemon? Why do the names have to be so cutesy?"

"Stop pretending you're so tough." Faye pushed Billie away with a swing of her hip and dipped her own paintbrush. "This is cute, Jenny. It'll cheer the living room right up."

"That's what I was thinking." Jenny put a foot on the lowest rung of the ladder to test for stability. She was looking forward to the change. "Maybe I'll buy a sewing machine and fabric or those stretch covers you can pull over old couches when I get my first paycheck."

"Good for you." Billie swiped a wide arc of paint across the wall and stepped back to check the effect.

"Well, well, well. Doesn't that look like the sun is about to rise in here?"

Faye stepped forward and swiped another arc on the wall, crossing Billie's.

"Jeez, Faye, that's my spot. Get your own." Billie tried to shove Faye back with her hip.

Faye laughed mischievously and danced out of reach. "Sorry, not sorry." She dipped her brush back in the paint can and started to pain, humming a tune under her breath.

Billie watched her for a moment, then turned back to her own section of the wall. "Jenny, do you have music? I can't stand it when Faye's humming. She can't hold a tune for the life of her."

"I can too." Faye reached over and crossed Billie's paint stroke again.

Started, Billie squealed. "Jenny! Make Faye go away."

"Quiet, children. The adult has to focus. What music do you like?"

"Jazz," Billie said. "But not too modern."

"Pop music," Faye said, louder. "Something cute and recent."

"Faye, pop? Really?" Billie shook her head. "Jenny, don't let her have any more coffee."

"Sorry." Jenny pointed out the open door to the patio table that was bending under the breakfast feast Jon had dropped off before going to work in the vineyard. "It's all out there. Coffee. Tea. Cocoa. By the way, remind me to tell Jon the baked oatmeal with peaches and vanilla cream was really good."

"I liked the bagel with lox," Billie said. "And the veggie frittatas. Did you eat anything, Faye?"

"Waffles with blueberry compote and yogurt, and as much French toast with fresh berries and whipped cream as would fit," Faye said happily. "And for your information, I had tea, not coffee. You're wrong *again.*"

Billie groaned. "She won't stop being weird, Jenny!"

"Okay, you two, that's enough. I'm putting on waltzes." Jenny opened a playlist on her phone and connected to the speaker she'd put on the piano. A gentle, lilting melody drifted through the room like a breath of fresh air. She closed her eyes and let the delicate twirls of the music guide her around the floor like the invisible hand of a dancer.

"Go, Jen!" Faye laughed.

Jenny opened her eyes and saw that Faye had joined her. Arms in the air, she was dancing, the paint brush high over her head and dripping lemon sugar on her tattered T-shirt.

"Nooo, come on! We'll never get this room done! I have a cormorant to feed!" Billie swiped at the wall.

"Join us!" Jenny laughed and twirled closer to Billie. Faye closed in from the other side, and between them, they herded Billie away from the wall and into the room.

"Oh, fine. One dance—then we paint."

"*First* we dance," Faye sang to the music. "Do it, Bills!"

Jenny twirled, grinning. "Yes, do it, Bills!"

Billie opened her arms wide, a paint roller in one hand and a ball of crumpled-up kitchen paper in the other. She closed her eyes and lay her head into her neck, then started twirling in wide circles, interrupted only by sidesteps when the music changed.

The music grew louder and wilder as the waltzes gathered momentum. They swirled together, laughing when they bumped into covered sofas and tables, but never stopping.

Lost in the music and the moment, humming, Jenny lifted her roller and began to paint in time with the rhythm. The others joined in, each with her own brush or roller, and soon they were dancing and painting together.

The living room and the long corridor were a mess of color and laughter, the walls alive with the vibrant new shade. With each stroke of the brush, they added to the energy of the room.

They drifted in and out as they pleased, painting and dancing, eating and drinking mimosas. Later, when it got hot outside and Polly started to bark for company and the tide lapped lazily out of the tide pools, they had icy lemonade and cream cakes.

Billie left to feed her bird, but Hannah and Jon stopped by with blackened salmon tacos and cilantro-lime slaw. After lunch, when their guests were gone, Jenny and Faye changed up the music, taped the rest of the crown molding, and resumed painting. Billie returned and helped. As the hours passed, the sun began to set, dipping the room into fiery shades of copper and red that glowed and shimmered in the new paint like pools of burnished gold and fire.

Finally, the women stepped back, admiring their work. Jenny was tired but satisfied with the new look.

"Wow," Billie breathed. "We did it."

"We did," Faye agreed, wiping her forehead and leaving a smudge of paint. "And it looks amazing."

Jenny put her roller in a bucket and wiped her hands on her rolled-up, paint-splattered jeans. "It's beautiful. I had no idea it would make this much of a difference. The room is officially transformed." This was the first house project she had done herself since leaving Nantucket. It was a new beginning.

Faye gave Jenny a knowing smile. "Feels good, doesn't it?" she said.

Jenny nodded, feeling a lump form in her throat. But they were no longer made of sandpaper, and she no longer had to swallow them back down. It dissolved on its own, riding the wake of a breath that had waited a long time to leave her body. "Yeah." Jenny exhaled, soft and long. "It feels good. It feels like this is my home. *My* home."

"It can be small, or it can be big, tasseled or lemon white—none of that matters as long as you feel you are home," Faye agreed softly.

Billie clapped her hands together, breaking the moment. "All right, ladies," she announced. "We're done for the day. There's only the bit behind the piano left, but we'll need Jon's and Michael's help to move it. That's for tomorrow."

Faye stretched, eyeing the leftover wall. Suddenly, a shiver ran over her as if an icy hand had touched her warm neck. "Brrr. *Again.*" She dropped her arms. "Hey, Jen," she said slowly. "Those sayings Rosie stitched."

Jenny came to stand beside her. "What about them?"

"Read them out loud for me," Faye said.

"Why?"

"Do it."

Jenny cleared her throat. " 'Kay. That one says *you can have your cake and eat it if you share.*"

"I remember her saying that one a lot," Billie said. "I still don't know what it means."

"I know." Jenny stepped closer to read the next one. "*Two birds of a feather flock together but sometimes fly apart.* I can't imagine how long it took to stitch that."

"It was her hobby. Like Jon can cook for hours without getting tired of it, and you can sit on the beach and stare at the ocean without your eyeballs drying up."

"I mean, I do blink. Okay. Next one says, *Better late than never, but earlier is best.*" She groaned, sounding much like Billie. "These are Grandma-level dad jokes. Of course, she thought they were hilarious."

Faye turned to read the next one. "*What doesn't kill you can still leave a few bruises.* And below, *The sky's the limit, but there's always a higher peak.*"

Jenny nodded. "*Don't count your chickens before they hatch, but do count your eggs.*" She shook her head. "So corny, Grandma."

Billie joined them too. "*An apple a day keeps the dentist away.* What? Why the dentist? Are apples good for your teeth? What about the fruit sugar?"

"Jenny, read the last one," Faye said.

"Billie did the last one," Jenny said, surprised. "There are no more sayings."

"There's one left." Faye pointed at the frame next to the empty spot where the pretty cove had hung.

"It's only my crooked letter," Jenny said slowly. "Oh. *Oh.*"

They all inhaled at the same time, and when they spoke, they spoke together. "*X always marks the spot.*"

Jenny wiped her hands one more time on her jeans. Then she reached past the grand piano and lifted the frame off its nail.

CHAPTER 36

H ow does it feel?" Faye asked breathlessly. "Did she hide something in it? Is something tucked into the frame?"

Jenny pressed a finger into the fabric. It was stiff with her clumsy childhood stitches and old age. "There's some give, but not enough for gems and doubloons." She looked up. "We're just being silly, right? What could my old X possibly mark?"

"If I remember correctly," Billie said and lifted a wise finger in the air, "we were rarely able to under-stand—far less predict—the workings of your grand-mother's mind. She was an enigma wrapped into a mystery."

"Oh, not you too with the corny sayings, Billie." This time, it was Faye who groaned. "Just open it al-ready, Jenny. We already learned that your grandmoth-er tucked a lot of things into places you knew noth-ing about. Let's see if she was serious about X always marking the spot. Maybe she tucked ten dollars under the stitching, waiting for you to figure it out."

"Ten dollars?" Billie sounded incredulous. "Ten dol-lars was a lot of money back then. She'd hardly have used that much when we were only wee little ones, using our pocket money to buy ye olde penny candy. Open it up to show Faye she's wrong." Billie, too, leaned forward to see.

"I can't." Jenny flipped the frame over. "I nailed the frame and fabric together good."

"Show me." Faye took the frame from Jenny and eagerly studied the back. "I think it might've been opened and nailed shut again, eh? Look at the nail holes there." She pointed.

Billie took the frame from her, equally unceremoniously. "That could be anything," she claimed. "Could be just Jenny and her two left hands. One wrong smack with the hammer, and you have yourself a hole like that."

Faye snatched the frame back and showed the holes to Jenny. "Accident or not? Do you remember?"Jenny had to laugh. She took the frame from Faye and laid it back on the piano. "Do I remember whether I smacked a nail the wrong way with my hammer thirty years ago? I think we'll just get pliers and pull out the nails to see."

Billie reached around Faye and pressed a finger in the middle of the X. "Bit squishy," she breathed. "Could be something in there, unless it's bunched-up fabric because Jen was too lazy to cut off the excess."

"Definitely a possibility," Jenny said mildly.

"That's way more squish than a ten-dollar bill makes." Faye clapped her hands. "I'm telling you, Rosie hid Jenny some tray-sure!"

Billie snapped her fingers as if she'd just had a major brain wave. "I know! It's ten dollars in one-dollar—" The chime of the doorbell interrupted her. She tilted her head, mouth still open. "Jen? Do you have a rendezvous with my dear brother I wasn't informed of?"

Jenny closed her eyes and opened them again. "I don't have rendezvous, my dear. Rendezvous are romantic. I'm not looking for romance. I only have dry, dusty *meetings*." She grinned. Like a besotted teenager, she'd played that half-kiss over in her memories in an endless loop.

"Yeah, I know, but still—" Again, the chime broke into Billie's sentence. She crossed her arms. "Are you so unavailable all of a sudden that he isn't even allowed in? He had lunch with us."

"The door would be open already if you'd stop talking for a moment." Jenny patted Billie's shoulder in passing.

She crossed the blue-green dappled foyer and opened the door.

In front of her stood Sebastian, a big white cake box in his hands. He smiled crookedly. "Hi," he said. "Is it a bad time?"

"No. No, come on in, Sebastian. I'm glad to see you."

"Thanks. I'm about to leave Mendocino Cove." Behind him stood a battered Toyota, loaded to the brim with suitcases and backpacks, a duvet and book boxes. "I stopped by to give you this." He held out his offering.

"You shouldn't have." Jenny took it. It was surprisingly heavy. "What's it for?"

"A thank-you for offering your map," he said, looking like River when his first patient had died. "I know you were throwing a drowning man a life preserver, and I appreciate it. Even if it didn't save me."

"Everything will be all right." Following an impulse, Jenny hugged her free arm around the young man. "Come on in, my dear."

For the blink of a garnet's wingbeat, the young man's mouth dipped and curled as if he was going to cry. Then he blushed a tender red and recovered his smile. "Thanks."

Jenny led the way, knowing he would follow her. He needed to talk one more time before leaving. She went into the kitchen and set the box on the counter. "What did you bring me?" she asked.

"It's a shipwreck cake," he said. "I read your paper on the whaler in Nantucket."

"Really?"

"I'm no baker, but I stayed up late figuring out how to make this cake for you. I didn't want to see anyone from the university, and I needed to keep busy. At least I wanted to do you a small favor, too."

Jenny looked at him, speechless for the moment. "Aww," she said then. "That's very...sweet of you." She winked. "Get it? Sweet?" She opened the box.

He smiled, a little less crooked than before. "Yeah, I get it. Funny. I hope you like chocolate. I don't know if you do—maybe I should have made it vanilla?"

"I love chocolate. Sebastian, this is adorable!" Jenny lifted out a flawlessly glazed cake with the tiny shipwreck of a whaling brig on top.

"Oh." He exhaled, relieved. "Oh good. It's a chocolate and salted caramel cake. The shipwreck is edible. I made it out of rice crisp and fondant. I watched a lot of tutorials to get it so it wouldn't fall apart." The words tumbled out of his mouth.

"And this?" Jenny turned the cake to see the other side. "Is this a treasure chest filled with gold sprinkles to resemble gold coins? Aww."

Sebastian nodded. "I half-sunk it into the cake. Buried treasure?" He glanced at her, a little flushed with pleasure that she liked the cake.

"Buried treasure." Jenny smiled at him, letting him see how much she appreciated his effort. "Thank you, Sebastian." She set the cake back down. "I already liked you before, but now we are friends."

He looked at his feet. When he looked back up, the shame was gone from his eyes and his gaze was open and clear. "Friends," he said quietly. "I like that."

"We have something else in common," she said.

"What's that?"

"We both needed a new beginning. We both get a second chance." She put a hand on his arm, feeling like she was talking to a son. "But the ending that comes first is hard and confusing and feels unfair, doesn't it?"

"A little," he admitted sheepishly. "I worked hard to be where I was. Though if I'm honest, I can't quite remember the last time I enjoyed myself. I was like a train, following the tracks and always stressed out. But I had a long talk with Dr. Perez. She made me see it in a different way. She made me see that it was stressful because I didn't enjoy what I was doing." He sighed. "And yet it somehow feels unfair. It was so much work to get the job."

"But listen—at least we get another beginning. We take it and run with it. All right?"

She anxiously waited for his answer, for a confirmation that he was going to take life by the horns.

If Stan had believed in second chances, maybe he would be here with her now.

Sebastian looked at her for a long time, as if he was trying to discern what her own unfair ending had been.

"Yes," he said finally. "I suppose we do take life by the horns and start over. I suppose it is good to get a second chance."

CHAPTER 37

H ey, it's the professor!" Billie had come into the kitchen, carrying a stack of plates to the sink. "Rough going in the old office, huh? How are you, sweet angel boy?" She put down her stack and lightly boxed the young man's arm as if he were her brother.

"Better for being called a sweet angel boy," Sebastian said dryly and rubbed his arm. "Please don't hurt me. I brought food."

"It's a shipwreck cake," Jenny explained. "Look. Treasure chest. The sprinkles are *doubloons*."

"That's too cute." Faye had joined them too. She reached up and put both hands on the young man's shoulders, staring straight into his eyes. "Are you okay?"

"I am." Sebastian bravely held the inquisitorial gaze. "I think."

Faye smiled and dropped down on her heels. "Good. Glad to hear. What are you going to do now? Do you know already?"

For a moment, he hesitated. "I have no idea."

"Well, what would you like to do? Apply at a different university and give it another go?"

"The new jobs don't come out until the fall. That's fine. I need a break. I'd like to do something outside. I used to be a guide for historical hiking tours as a student. It doesn't pay much, but maybe I'll get back to it while I figure things out."

Faye put her head to the side. "So you're fit, you have a degree, and you want to do something outside, be in nature while preserving history and cultural heritage?"

"That sounds perfect," Sebastian admitted. "I even did my thesis in environmental history."

"Billie?" Faye asked. "Could you help?"

"I can? Oh. Maybe I can!"

Faye nodded. "We have a friend who's a senior park ranger in Yosemite."

Jenny caught the slight pause before the word friend. "Who is that, Faye?"

"Lex. My cousin, Lex," Billie cut in and shook her head at Jenny behind Faye's back.

Lex was the twin Faye had been engaged to. Yet she had been the one to think of him, not his cousin, Billie.

"If you want, I'll put in a word for you," Billie said. "They're hiring right now."

Sebastian's eyes widened. "Really?" he said, and Jenny thought there was more animation on the young man's face than she'd ever seen before.

Billie nodded. "I'll ask Lex to get in touch with you. You'll have to ace some tests and interviews and all that, but I think you would be a great fit for the job. See what goes since you're taking the summer off, anyway.

If it doesn't work out, fine. At least you will know if it's an option."

Sebastian shook his head as if there was no chance that he wouldn't love the job. "I'll leave for Yosemite tonight! I can be there before midnight."

"I'll call him right now. He said they're still interviewing." Billie pulled out her phone and wrote a text, casually wandering out of the kitchen.

"Whoa. Did that just happen?" Sebastian was beaming. "Man, am I glad I made that cake!"

Both Jenny and Faye laughed. "It's just an interview," Faye said. "And Lex can be tough to please."

"Even if you get it, it'll probably be an entry-level job," Jenny added.

"I've never had anything but an entry-level job," Sebastian said cheerfully. "I'll give it a shot!"

"Yep." Billie came back in, waving her phone. "Lex will meet you the day after tomorrow, and he sent the address of a place where you can stay. I'll text you the details if you give me your number."

Sebastian pulled out his phone. "Thank you. I appreciate it."

"You're welcome." Billie copied his number, her fingers flying over the keys as she sent him the details of his job interview. "It'll be a big change from teaching."

"That's exactly what I want."

"Well then, congratulations! I hope it works out and you love being a ranger," Jenny said. "Should we celebrate with cake?" She lifted the masterpiece out of the box and set it on a pretty blue glass stand. "Hang on."

She snapped a photo of it and sent it to Audrey and River. "Audrey has her last exam today," she said in a manner of explanation. "And River has worked for two solid days without any sleep. I've been sending them both little messages all day long. Not sure if they're helpful or annoying, but I thought it couldn't hurt to remind them that I love them."

"That never hurts," Faye agreed. "Definitely send them pictures of a shipwreck cake."

"So do we eat it now?" Billie wanted to know. "If you're just taking photos of it, I'll go talk to my cormorant. She's back in shape, and I have to let her go tomorrow."

"Of course we eat now." Jenny grabbed clean plates from the cabinet. One of the advantages of living in a former hotel was the abundant supply of clean china, silverware, and glasses. "How about the beach?"

They carried out trays with plates and forks, glasses of milky coffee, and matches to light the bonfire. Dry driftwood was plentiful on the beach. Jenny watched Sebastian run around, hauling over more than they needed. She spotted Faye watching him too, a content expression on her face. Soon, they had started a sparkling, crackling bonfire and sat on the logs to eat cake and talk about the future.

"I haven't gone back to the department," Sebastian said. He was sitting beside Jenny. "I was too embarrassed to show my face after the talk with Dr. Perez." He set down his plate beside him on the sun-bleached, dry log. "I still hear things through the grapevine, though."

"Like?" Jenny looked up.

The shadows of the fire danced across his face when he smiled. "Like you are going to teach a couple of classes for the department."

"Time for *me* to thank *you*." She smiled back at him. "Thank you for mentioning my degree and showing Carolina my papers."

"To be honest, it was an afterthought," Sebastian admitted. "I needed a moment to recover from learning my tenure was officially off the table. But once the shock settled, I thought at least I might be able to get you a foot in the door."

"That was very kind of you. I enjoyed teaching, but I had no idea anyone would still consider me after so many years of not working."

"Maybe it's like biking," Sebastian said. "I never learned how to be a good teacher, but I can see you walk into a lecture hall and talk to everyone as if it's no big deal."

"It's been a hot minute since I last did that." She smiled nervously at the image.

"Caroline thinks you are more than qualified," Sebastian said reassuringly. Like all of them, he'd taken off his shoes and was barefoot. He dug his toes in the sand. "She was really taken with the love story between William Langley and his sweetheart. What was her name?"

"Phoebe Seabrook. It was an unusual name back then. But it fit her well—she was an unusual young woman."

"Do you know more about their story?"

"I lost their trail, unfortunately. There were no proper records since William had basically stolen the ship. I'm afraid they drowned when their ship sank on the journey back to Nantucket."

"Maybe they drowned." Sebastian nodded thoughtfully. "But maybe they lived. If you're interested in doing more research in this direction—I think next fall, when my position will be open again, you have a real shot at getting it."

"Do you mind?"

He looked at her, and even in the dancing light of the fire, she could see the smile in his eyes. "I'd rather you get it than anyone else."

She nodded. "Thank you. I didn't want you to think that I was making a play for it."

"Well, you didn't. I claim some credit for that happening, though Carolina would have found you on her own. Not much escapes that woman."

"You get all the credit," Jenny said. "Without you, I would've taken a job at the supermarket."

"The students already took all the jobs at the supermarket." He laughed. "But the department wants your maritime expertise. Just one little publication about Will and Phoebe in the next year to show them you remember how to write a paper, and they'll be head over heels. Even if it's just an article in the Cove Chronicle."

"I'll try," Jenny said. "I'm not sure I have anything more to add. I checked all the records I could think of for their names. Besides, Nantucket is far away. I have no money to go back." She shrugged.

"Well, it doesn't have to be about Will and Phoebe. You do have the map. It might not tie in with your other work, but who knows? Maybe it's even more interesting."

Jenny nodded. Nothing would ever touch her heart like the two unlucky teenage lovers from Nantucket. "I'll count on that. Thanks, Sebastian."

"My new beginning wouldn't be as good without yours," he said and touched his elbow to hers in a gesture of comradery. "We'll talk," he promised. "I'll email and tell you about my quick procession through the ranks."

"I'll do the same." The moon had risen, a golden sickle in a velvety sky, and the ocean rushed its eternal lullaby. Jenny stretched; she was ready to go in, to cuddle up with a blanket on the sofa and watch something silly and lighthearted on her phone.

She glanced at her friends to see how they were doing and grinned.

Faye was teasing Billie again, laughing behind her hand while Billie looked outraged, arguing some point Faye had only made to provoke her friend.

"Jenny?" Sebastian stood and shook the sand off his jeans.

"Yeah?"

"Would you be mad if I asked to see your scrimshaw tooth? I've never seen one outside a museum."

"Sure. Give me a minute, I'll go get it."

CHAPTER 38

Jenny went inside where the whale tooth lay in the armoire, protected by the good tablecloths. She washed her hands and wrapped the tooth into a clean, dry towel, then brought it outside.

"Wow. It's bigger than the ones I've seen." He pointed the flashlight of his phone at the tooth to supplement the flickering light from the fire. "There's a whole story carved on it."

"That's what I believe. It starts here, at the very bottom." Jenny pointed to a miniature ship in full sail. "I think it shows a whaler leaving port. Those lines here are houses, don't you think? And the ship's bow is pointing away from them."

"Yes, you're right." Sebastian turned the tooth. The images wound their way upward like the leaves on a vine. "This carving is next. What is it?"

"I can't tell. A crooked cup? A wiggly necklace?"

Sebastian leaned closer. "It's Cape Horn," he said suddenly. "See?" He traced the shape with a finger just above the scrimshaw.

"Of course." Excitement suddenly fluttered in Jenny's throat. She put a hand on the spot. "You're right. Someone rounded Cape Horn."

Their eyes met.

"They came from the East Coast," Jenny said out loud what they both thought. "Since this is a whale tooth, they were probably whalers, coming from Boston, or New York, or Baltimore." She took a breath, all sleepiness gone. "They could even have come from Nantucket. Did you know my family is originally from Nantucket?"

"Is that why you did your PhD there?"

"Sort of. My grandmother liked the idea of us going back." She pointed at the scrimshaw. "What's the next carving?"

Again, Sebastian turned the tooth a fraction, and they put their heads together to study it. The next images were a little higher, spiraling toward the tip. "A tree. And beside it is a...head? Is that supposed to be hair? There are no features. Is it a monkey?"

For a moment, they both stared at the carving. Jenny ran a finger over the streaks and lines, as if she could feel what it was supposed to be. "It's a palm tree," she said finally. "The round thing could be a coconut."

"A coconut. Yes, of course." Sebastian squinted. "They were somewhere where the scrimshaw artist saw coconuts on palm trees."

"A lot of eastern whalers stopped by the Pacific islands for food and water," Jenny confirmed. "Will and Phoebe's ship landed in Hawaii."

"Hawaii has plenty of coconut palms." Sebastian chuckled. "It was Will who carved the scrimshaw."

"Who says it wasn't Phoebe?" Jenny smiled. "Knowing her, she probably wielded a knife as well as her man."

"Yes, why not? And why assume they drowned? Maybe they decided not to return to Nantucket and their angry families and instead came here. Maybe they, just like us, wanted a fresh start."

"Sure." Jenny chuckled at the thought. "And I, a historian researching their doomed love affair, just happened to find it in my grandmother's house."

"Even if it wasn't Will or Phoebe... Since the tooth belonged to your grandmother, it could have been carved by someone in your family." Sebastian picked up a handful of sand and let it run through his fingers. "It's the most straightforward way to explain how it came to be in your grandmother's armoire."

"But what if she found it at a flea market?"

He smiled. "That's possible, too."

Jenny nodded. There were so many heirlooms with nautical themes in the armoire. When did Grandma go out to all these alleged flea markets to find them? She didn't even like leaving the hotel, let alone Mendocino Cove...

"If your family really came from Nantucket, it was even likely they were involved in whaling since it was the dominant industry." Sebastian cleared his throat. "Do you know anything about a Nantucket branch?"

"No, nothing at all. I don't even know if there really is a connection. Maybe my grandmother just wanted one because she liked the pictures in a magazine or something. She would have thought nothing of making it up." Jenny chuckled. "I did look up my great-grandmother Magda's surname, which was Malihin. There never lived a single person with that name on Nantucket or Cape Cod." Jenny threw a twig into the crackling fire. "Besides, Magda lived here, not in Nantucket. I just found a picture of her in a photo album." She took the whale tooth from Sebastian, turning it as she followed the story from port to palm trees again. "A whaler traveling to the Pacific Ocean," she murmured.

"Did that happen a lot? It seems like a far journey."

"Yes, lots of whalers rounded Cape Horn and hunted in the Pacific. That's where the big whales were. It was worth the effort."

"Or maybe they just all wanted to escape the long Massachusetts winters, like normal people." Sebastian grinned. "Look, there's more. What's the next picture?"

"Hm. A small ship. And the face of a woman." A mischievous smile played on the woman's lips.

"It's beautiful," Sebastian said. "It has your eyes."

She turned to him. "Are you flirting with me?"

"No! It's just something about the eyes!" He held his open palms up.

"I don't know. Then there's another squiggly line. Another coast? I don't recognize the outline. Maybe it's their best guess at the coast of California?" He switched off his flashlight. "After all, someone dropped the tooth off over here."

"It's possible." Jenny rubbed her eyes and blinked back at the fire. It had burned down, and the moon cast silver light on the beach. Polly and her four best friends were sleeping near the rocks, their sleek coats shining like selkie hair.

Jenny wrapped the whale tooth back up. "Someone sailed from the East Coast around Cape Horn. They landed on an island with coconut palm trees, where they changed ships. The sailor was thinking of his sweetheart, maybe even someone he left in Nantucket. He sailed along a new coast, possibly landing in San Francisco, and sold his scrimshaw."

Sebastian nodded. "Keep the tooth safe. It might be valuable."

"I'm starting to think it is." She would take up Carolina's offer and store it at the university. "How much is it worth, do you think?"

"I won't pretend I didn't look it up when Carolina mentioned it. Sheer curiosity, of course. Now that I have seen how intricate the carving is, I'd say it's in the upper range the internet claims."

"Which is?"

"Several thousand to tens of thousands of dollars, depending on things like quality, historical significance, and market demand. I'd say this one ranks way up there. I saw smaller ones auction off for seventy-five, eighty thousand." He smiled.

"Eighty *thousand*? American dollars? Huh." Jenny stared at the lumpy bundle on her knees. "Golly, as Grandma would have said. She must've had no idea."

"She knew enough to keep it with the good table-cloths, not blazing bonfires," Billie pointed out. She and Faye had joined them a while ago, listening quietly.

"Maybe the tablecloths are only in the armoire to protect things," Faye pointed out. "You need to take them all out super carefully and check for more treasure."

Sebastian switched off the flashlight on his phone and put it in his pocket. Then he stood, holding out his hand.

Jenny stood too.

"I should be off," he said. "I have a long drive ahead of me. Thank you for everything. I hope you do well."

"You too." Jenny shook his hand. "Stay in touch, Sebastian. We're friends now. One day, we'll meet at another beach bonfire to talk more about the mysteries of history and second chances."

"I'd like that," he said simply.

"Take care." Faye hugged Sebastian. "Good luck getting the job. Lex will help you get started."

"Thank you for thinking of him and the job. I owe you a big one." He took Faye's hand and bowed politely over it, blowing an air kiss. "I hope we will meet again, too."

"Well, you don't have to thank me." Billie held out her hand, and Sebastian took it. "I didn't really do anything."

"You called your cousin and put in a good word for me." He smiled. "Besides, I wouldn't have met any of you if it hadn't been for you inviting us to sit with you in the winery," Sebastian said. "I'm very grateful you did."

"Oh good. I'm glad you see it like that." Billie gave his hand a hearty shake. "You'll turn out all right yet."

Sebastian grinned and picked up his plate and glass. "Bye." He stepped over the log and walked back to the hotel.

"Yeah, he's all right now," Billie said, looking after him. They talked a while longer—so much had happened. Then Billie stood and brushed the sand off her jeans. "The fire is going out, and I should take off. Are you okay with the dishes, Jen?"

"Of course." Jenny stood to hug Billie. "Thanks, Bills. I'll see you soon."

"I could come tomorrow to help paint the last wall."

"You're always welcome to stop by, but no worries if you can't make it. It's only one more wall."

Billie waved and took off.

"Painting was a success, Jenny." Faye delicately cleared her throat. "But it's only cosmetic. You should have the foundation and wood checked out. Better safe than sorry."

"That's a kettle of fish for which I need Georgie's permission—and her money," Jenny said.

"It's your hotel too," Faye said and stood to gather the leftovers. "Maybe not on paper, but in essence. Ask your aunt to let you oversee renovations. You could cover the cost by selling a few of the heirlooms."

"Maybe." Jenny started to throw sand on the last embers of the fire. It hissed and crackled and died. "I will ask Aunt Georgie sometime. She's about as slippery as a jellyfish when it comes to the hotel."

"She doesn't have to do anything, and you're her niece. I think she owes you a few minutes on the phone and a decision." Faye picked up the cake stand and the last of the glasses. "Let's go inside."

Jenny took a full basket in one hand and safely tucked her wrapped scrimshaw under her other arm, away from buttercream and doubloon sprinkles. "What a day," she remarked as they walked back to the house across the moonlit quicksilver sand.

"Things have become much more interesting since you came back," Faye replied. "Don't go away again."

"I have a house, and I have a wonderful job. Audrey wants to come visit after the exams are over." Jenny sighed. "I'm so glad they don't have to worry about me anymore. But I still haven't told the kids about Stan's business."

"That's another story for another day," Faye said and stopped on the terrace. A light breeze swayed the fronds of the potted ferns, and the sound of the sea caressed them like the hand of a mother. "We forgot."

"What?" Jenny stopped too.

"Sebastian's visit sidetracked us." Faye shook back her hair, her eyes glinting in the moon. "Let's get pliers and open the frame where X marks the spot."

Jenny laughed; she'd completely forgotten about their treasure map and the prospect of an Easter egg ten-dollar bill. She hitched the scrimshaw higher in her arm and stepped into the living room.

Inside, the hotel smelled like lemon paint and friendship, laughter and dancing. The door to the armoire stood open again, as if it was asking for its whale tooth back.

"Is that a yes?" Faye came after her. "Don't tell me you're too tired. I'm not waiting until tomorrow."

Jenny laughed again. She set down the basket and returned the tooth to its rightful spot, tightly closing the armoire and giving it an extra pat for good measure. Then she turned to her friend. "Isn't that also another story for another day?"

"No." Faye smiled. "Nice try. That's definitely still this story."

"Then I'm not too tired. Let's go get a pair of pliers. Who knows? We might find even more buried treasure today."

CHAPTER 39

The soft morning sea breeze tugged on the table-cloth. Billie smoothed it back in place and smiled across the breakfast table.

"Thank you for including me in the treasure hunt," she said politely. "I'd hate to wake up to find you opened the frame without me."

Jenny smiled back. It had seemed like a good idea last night to open the frame. Luckily for her and Faye, Grandma's only pair of pliers broke on the first nail, snapping clean in two when the rusted pivot screw gave out. "Thank *you*, Billie, for making another spectacular breakfast," she said primly. "And for also inviting your brother."

"And his pliers," Faye added sweetly, pouring coffee.

Jon crossed his arm, amused. "I'm just glad to be included in anything at all. Even if it's only so you can borrow my tools."

"We also very much enjoy your company." Jenny glanced at him and smiled. She still felt his kiss and remembered his words on that magical tour of the vineyard.

He winked at her. "Well then, that's good. How's the bike holding up?"

"Um. It has a flat tire. I ran over a broken shell."

"Should I stop by to fix it?" he offered.

"I can do it, Jon. But thank you very much," she said. She had to get used to doing her own honey-do list.

"And in order to do it yourself, do you need to borrow any of my tools?" he asked good-humoredly.

Jenny had no idea what tools she needed. "Maybe?"

He grinned and picked up his mug. "Let me know when you figure it out."

The steam mingled with the fog that wafted around the dock like the fluffy walls of a room. They could only see each other and the food on the table. Jenny glanced at it. She was hungry. All that painting and dancing the day before had burned calories.

"So what do we get for brekkie?" She unrolled her napkin and smoothed it over her knees.

"Ah. Billie and I wanted to change it up just a little," Jon said and leaned forward to inspect the table. "Those are French toast roll-ups filled with cream and berries."

"Yummy." Faye pulled her chair closer.

"He made those for you," Billie mentioned. "You always liked them."

"I did. I do. Thanks very much, Jon." Faye speared one and pulled it unceremoniously onto her plate.

"You're welcome," Jon said. "Billie made savory waffles with cheese and bacon, and what, oatmeal pancakes, right?"

"Yes. Try them with cherry compote and powdered sugar, Jenny."

"Don't mind if I do." Jenny helped herself. Her stomach was growling, yet she ate more in a week in Mendocino Cove than in a month in Portland.

"I'll have avocado toast with peaches and see how it goes," Billie announced. "Sometimes, you have to strike out to reach new shores."

"I agree," Jon said. "I already ate while I was cooking, by the way. Apple waffles with cinnamon. They were good."

Faye squinted into the dense fog on the water as if the apple waffles might have gotten stuck in it. "Where are they? Did you eat all of them? Are there more?"

Jon's eyes twinkled. "There's an enormous stack in Billie's kitchen. I thought I brought out enough food, but I'm happy to get more."

"Faye, you're fine! The table is practically bowing with food." Billie took a bite of her avocado toast. "Huh. Interesting." She took another bite. "Jon, if you're not eating—would you open up the frame for us?"

"Yup." He held out a hand. "Give it."

Jenny pulled the crookedly stitched X from the straw purse hanging on the back of her chair and handed it over. "There you go."

"Let's see." He inspected the frame and whistled through his teeth. "You sure didn't do things by half as a kid, did you?"

"I didn't want Grandma to take it out and send me back to fix all the crooked bits," Jenny explained.

"Though the hope is that she opened it, put a little treat for me inside, nailed it shut again, and waited to see if I'd figure it out. Of course, it's not likely she did. It's probably empty." She had the feeling she got on the rare occasions she bought a lottery ticket. Of course, it wasn't likely. Of course, she would check the numbers anyway, when they came out.

"Either way, it's some solid craftsmanship." Jon pulled pliers from his pocket and wrestled a grip on a flat nail head. Sometimes the pliers slipped, but one by one, he popped the nails off the frame, growing a pile of them on his plate.

"Here you go." He handed the loose frame back to Jenny.

"Thank you, Jon." Their hands met.

A bolt of lightning shot through Jenny. Jon looked at her, his eyes darkening with a flash of desire that she recognized immediately in herself.

"Oh!" Jenny pulled away, startled.

"Sorry." Jon blew out a long breath. "I'm not grounded."

"No, it's—it's fine."

"Uh. What's going on?" Faye looked back and forth between Jenny and Jon. Suddenly, she flinched. "Ow! *What?* Why are you kicking me?"

"I'm not. You knocked against the table." Billie grinned widely and pointed at the frame. "Open that thing, Jenny."

"Trying to." Jenny, cheeks warm despite the morning cool, wiggled on the frame until it came loose. Gently, she lifted it off.

"Treasure. I'm telling you." Faye bit into a pancake and chewed excitedly.

Jenny laid the stitched letter face down on the table. "The extra fabric is folded in the back. It's been pressed together so hard for so long it's practically glued together." She tried to pry off a corner with her fingernail, but her fingernails were always cut short. A quick glance confirmed the same applied to her friends. "I don't want to rip it open."

"The pliers are too blunt. Do you have a fine pair of scissors, Billie?" Jon asked. "Or a scalpel?"

"I only have kitchen and gardening scissors," Billie said. "The bigger, the better."

"Faye—I still have the sewing scissors you gave me." Jenny had forgotten about them, but she'd been carrying the small scissors in her purse ever since she'd been to Faye's store. "Here." She fished them out of the side pocket. The fine tip made exactly the shallow cuts she needed. Carefully, she unfolded the fabric. "I see something."

"What?" Everyone leaned in.

Jenny's hands shook a little. She tucked the scissors back in her purse and took a deep breath. "It's paper. It's folded paper."

"It's a letter," Billie said softly.

As gently as she could, Jenny pulled out the paper. The edge crumbled, and a little bit of the letter was lost.

"It's so fragile." Luckily, the breeze had calmed. Even the sea seemed to be holding her breath.

"Is it from your grandma?" Faye asked. "Did Rosie write it?"

"Hm." Jenny barely breathed for fear the paper would fall apart in her hands. "No, it's old. Really old." A moment ago, she felt warm from Jon's touch. Now, she felt cold with nerves. "Guys. Let's bring this inside. I'm scared it will crumble if the breeze returns. Careful. Careful."

"Here." Jon pushed the nails off his plate and handed it to Jenny. "Slide it on there. You can carry it without touching it."

Jenny did as he said. They hurried off the dock and brought the letter into Billie's cottage.

"Put it on the table by the bay window," Billie said and shoved her animal lover and cooking magazines aside.

Jenny set down the plate and took a seat in front of it.

CHAPTER 40

F aye had brought the embroidery and laid it beside the plate. "I think there is another piece of paper in there," she said. "The paper looks brighter than what you pulled out."

"Yes, you're right." Jenny wiggled the note out, relieved at how sturdy the paper was. She unfolded it without a problem and cleared her throat to read out loud.

"I found a letter in my mother's old things this morning and thought of you, Jenny. Did I tell you Magda was born on a ship and believed in the kraken? You are so much like her, besides believing in the kraken, which, of course, does not exist.

I'm afraid the letter will fall apart if I send it in the mail or that Georgie will get it first and throw it away. I'm putting it in a spot where only you would look and trust that if Mom wants you to have the letter, she'll remind you that X always marks the spot. Though, of course, ghosts don't exist, either. Chin up, kiddo. I love you. We'll have a bonfire again sometime, somewhere, in a place where it's nice and warm and the raccoons can't open the bins."

Jenny stopped and swallowed.

I love you too, Grandma.

"There's more." Billie pointed.

Jenny read on. *"PS Nice job nailing the frame shut. No matter what Clarissa says, I have not a spot of arthritis, yet it took me a whole week to open it."*

For a moment, there was silence.

Then Faye said, "Clarissa is my mom. Of *course* Rosie had arthritis in her hands."

Jenny put down the note and turned to the faint ink marks on the old letter. She would savor her grandmother's note later, when she was alone. "Grandma left me a letter that Magda's *mom* wrote to Magda. No wonder the paper is brittle. Do we have more light? It's still foggy outside."

"What's the kraken again?" Billie switched on a floor lamp and bent it to shine on the table. "I know it's an enormous octopus, but what's the story behind it?"

Jon was already scrolling on his phone. "The internet says it's an unconfirmed cephalopod. Ha. Sounds about right."

"Read the old letter, Jenny," Faye said with shining eyes.

"My heart is beating hard." Jenny smiled nervously. "I feel like Grandma is standing next to me." She tilted the plate for the light to hit the faded words at the best angle and read.

"I will sail tomorrow, my sweet Magda. Your dear father has the sea in his blood, and it calls to him." She

stopped and pressed a hand to her warm cheek. "I can't read the next line. It's right in the crease."

"Is there more that you can read?" Billie asked.

"There is." Jenny moved on. "*I trust your beloved husband will keep you and my precious granddaughter safe while we are away from home. Your dear father and I won't be long—he plans only a short sail to take the air, to enjoy a seabound view of the coast he surveyed so carefully, and to remember the anniversary of our wedding. We are old, and it may be the last we have together on this earth, so you will forgive us for eloping once again, my dear. It is not a wish to hide, but only lasting marital love that joins our hands and hearts in this last, private adventure.*"

"Eloping?" Jon looked at Jenny.

"Yes." Jenny's breath shook on the way into her lungs.

"Oh," Faye said. "Her husband surveyed the coast? Because of the map we found in—"

"Yes." This time, Jenny only managed a whisper. "Let me read the rest."

"Do it." Billie patted her back.

"*If your husband asks where we are, tell him whatever tale will calm his poor nerves best. Suggest a visit to the city, perhaps. I trust we will be back before he finds that neither buggy nor horse are missing from our stable.*"

Billie giggled, and Jon shook his head. "No wonder the man's nerves were shot," he murmured.

Jenny adjusted the lamp. "*The sea was as blue on our wedding day as it is today, my dear. But she is a fickle*

*friend and full of unplumbed creatures. I have seen her
swallow many a good friend and brother to satisfy her
sheer whim of the moment. I don't mean to alarm you,
but should the sea claim Captain Langley and me—"*

"Langley?" Faye whispered. "Wasn't that William's
last name?"

*"—you will find exotic treasure hidden among the
cloth and linen in the new armoire. It is there for your
profit should you lose your beloved husband or otherwise fall on hard times. I left home with not a penny to
my name, and indeed, bearing the heavy debt of a ship.
I swore that no daughter of mine would ever again feel
that burden and that my child, and my child's children
forever on, would be safe and supported. Therefore,
do not hesitate to sell what I've collected on my jour-
neys—I did so only for the sake of my family. I still long
for my Nantucket. Let losing house and home never be
your fate."*

Jenny stopped reading out loud. But her eyes lingered
on the last lines.

*I will see you before long, my beloved Magda. Kiss
little Rosamunde's blooming cheeks from both me and
your dear father, Captain Langley.*

Forever yours, with eternal and motherly love,

Phoebe Seabrook Langley

Jenny looked up.

"Phoebe Seabrook was your great-great-grandmoth-
er," Faye whispered.

Jenny could barely believe the words. "And Magda
was William's and Phoebe's *daughter*." She fell back

into her chair, driving her fingers into her hair. "What are the chances I ended up researching the elopement of *my own ancestors?*" Her thoughts whirled.

Faye sat in a chair and took Jenny's hands in hers. "Rosie knew there was a family connection."

"Nantucket is a small island, and you are the descendant of not only one but two families who lived there. You were practically bound to come across your ancestors, researching anything at all," Billie said.

"Why did Grandma never tell me?"

"Maybe Magda didn't want her daughter to know that her grandparents stole a ship and eloped," Billie said. "Besides, I don't know the names of my great-great-grandparents, either. Few people do."

"You're right," Jenny said. She shook her head. "At least she left me the letter."

"Let's tuck it somewhere safe." Billie emptied a flat, smooth cardboard box of bird magazines and handed it to Jenny.

"You finally have the end to your story." Jon smiled. "I think Rosie just handed you a way to get your dream job."

Faye picked up Rosie's note and turned it around. "There's something scribbled on the back of Rosie's note."

"Read it," Jenny said, busy transferring the fragile older letter into the box.

"Okay. It says: *In case you are wondering, they came back. And as usual, they had a blast.*"

Laughter bubbled out of Jenny, as unexpected as the letter itself. Her friends joined her, laughing more at her outburst than the stunning news, but it didn't matter.

"I really have to tell Aunt Georgie about this," Jenny said when the bubbles finally calmed. She closed the lid over Phoebe's letter and put a hand on the box.

"There is one last sentence, Jenny. Listen." Faye was grinning from ear to ear and read, "*Since Georgie's husband already left her a fortune and the hotel has appreciated in value since you received your share, the collection in the armoire is yours. Tell that daughter of mine I said so.*"

"Oh boy," Jenny said. "Uh..."

"No, that's good, Jenny," Billie said cheerfully. "That's really, really good."

Jon came to stand beside her and put a hand on her shoulder. It felt grounding, and safe, and sweet. She looked up at him.

"Talk to your aunt," he said. "Give yourself a day before you call. Or ten, or twenty. There's no rush. All that can be a story for another day."

"I will do that." Jenny stood, put her arms around his neck, and laid her head on his shoulder. Some stories could wait. Others had to be told now, before it was too late.

Billie gasped, and Faye laughed with surprise. But Jon pressed a kiss on her forehead and pulled Jenny into an embrace that warmed her soul until she was filled only with love for him and wonder and joy, deep

and delicious, that she should be related to the stormy
young couple she loved so much.

They loved her too.

All this time, they had loved her.

Thank you for reading The Hotel at Beach and Forgotten. *Read the next book in the series,* The Store of
Love and Loss, *to stay in beautiful Mendocino Cove
and continue the saga!*

THE MENDOCINO COVE SERIES

A gorgeous feel-good series with wonderful characters! Four friends are taking a second chance on love and life as they start over together in the small town of Mendocino Cove. Set at the breathtakingly beautiful coast of Northern California, where the golden hills are covered in wildflowers, vineyards grow sweet grapes, and the coast is rugged and wild.

THE BAY HARBOR BEACH SERIES

★★★★★ *"Wonderfully written story. Rumors abound in this tale of loves and secrets."*

Lose yourself in this riveting feel-good saga of old secrets and new beginnings. Best friends support each other through life's ups and downs and matters of the heart as they boil salt water taffy, browse quaint stores for swimsuits, and sample pies at the Beach Bistro!

THE BEACH COVE SERIES

★★★★★ *"What an awesome series! Captivated in the first sentence! Beautiful writing!"*

Maisie returns to charming Beach Cove and meets a heartwarming cast of old friends and new neighbors. The beaches are sandy and inviting, the sea is bluer than it should be, and the small town is brimming with secrets! Together, Maisie and her best friends take turns helping each other through emotional trials, bittersweet mysteries, and matters of the heart.

About the Author

Nellie Brooks writes feel-good friendship fiction for women. You'll find flawed, likable characters who bake cakes and adopt animals, gorgeous coastal settings that will make you study your tea leaves for the next vacation date, a bunch of secrets that are best solved together, and happy endings until every last estranged friend and distant sister is safely back in the arms of her small town community!

Visit www.nelliebrooks.com to subscribe to her newsletter and hear about new releases and whatever else she has to say (not much usually since she's busy writing and studying her own tea leaves for vacations). You can also follow Nellie on Facebook and BookBub.

22969448R00174